The Right Hand of Velachaz

Rie Sheridan Rose

ISBN 978-1-77400-040-3 Ebook
ISBN 978-1-77400-039-7 Paperback

DEDICATION
This book is dedicated to my original trio of readers:
Christa, Chris and Mallory.
I thank you all.

CHAPTER 1

Street Rat

"This way! I saw him go down that alley."

"We'll show him."

"Split up. You go that way—"

The voices faded in the distance, calling back and forth as they went.

Teman crouched behind a rough stone wall, trying to control his panting as he squinted into the golden rays of the setting sun. He didn't spy any of the pack of boys who had been chasing him since they spotted him scrabbling through a rubbish bin at nooning. From the sound of things, maybe he had finally lost them—he'd been dodging through the back streets for hours now.

Planting his back against the wall, he closed his eyes and tried to remember a time when he wasn't hungry and cold. He couldn't do it. Even before he had found himself living by his wits on the streets of Farlea, life had been a hard row to hoe. His family had little to begin with and, as Teman grew, that little had stretched too thin.

His exhaustion would have worried him if he'd had the energy to spare, but at the moment, all he could concentrate on was finding a safe place to spend the night. Hopefully beyond the reach of the band of boys who'd been chasing him.

Teman sighed and opened his eyes. With a gasp of shock, he tried to back through the stone wall at the sight of a robed figure looming before him.

The figure smiled, a twinkling glimmer lighting its dark eyes. "Don't be afraid, little mouse. I don't wish to harm you."

"B-but you're—"

"'The terribly wicked wizard, Velachaz'. Yes, I know. How about some dinner?"

Teman swallowed hard at the very mention of food. He'd found a crust of bread in the marketplace yesterday evening, and it had seemed a feast. Today the boys had rousted him from his search before he found even a crumb. But to trust the magic-user...

"Come, boy. If you follow me, I can promise you a hot meal and a soft bed for the night."

The last offer was too tempting to ignore. There had been a great many nights spent under bridges or inside stables lately—when he was lucky. More nights than he could count had been spent curled against a wall or in an open field. If necessary, he could always run away...probably.

Steeling his courage, Teman nodded and got to his feet. Heart in his throat, he followed the mysterious wizard. As they wound their way quickly through the maze of streets making up the slums of Farlea, the boy studied the figure before him curiously.

Velachaz wore a velvet cloak of deepest midnight over a robe that shimmered and shifted in color when the boy tried to identify its hue. The mage's hair was black as coal, except for a silver streak that ran along his right temple, and his beardless features were neither young nor old. On his left hand, a heavy silver ring with a blue stone began to glow, dimly at first, and then brighter and brighter as the sunlight faded, illuminating the street around them.

Teman noticed the magic with unease, and he had second thoughts about the wisdom of his decision to follow Velachaz. He began to slow his steps, gradually falling further and further behind the wizard, his gaze darting right and left as he searched for an alley to duck into.

All at once, Velachaz spun abruptly, gesturing toward Teman, and muttering something under his breath. The boy found himself frozen where he stood, unable to move. His heart skipped a beat, but he faced the magician bravely.

"Don't look so terrified, little mouse." Velachaz's stern face was transformed by the gentle smile Teman had seen earlier. "You have been through a great deal, haven't you," he murmured softly. "What has put the shadows in your eyes?"

He uttered a harsh command.

Teman slid to the cobblestones, his legs no longer willing to hold him up.

Velachaz hunkered down in the dirt beside the boy, ignoring the trailing velvet of his cloak. "I don't wish to harm you, lad. You have my word. Someday, you will have to trust someone. It may as well be today. Come." He held out his ringed hand, and Teman tentatively took it.

The wizard pulled him to his feet. "Tonight: dinner and rest. Tomorrow, if you are willing, perhaps I may have a task for you..."

There it was—the hidden thorn in this rose. No one had ever offered him anything for free.

Velachaz waved a hand before the blank wall of the nondescript building beside them, and a wooden door appeared. The wizard flung it open and gestured Teman inside with a flourish. "Welcome to my home."

Teman stepped forward, mouth hanging open in awe. The single room contained jumbled mounds of objects everywhere he turned. It was crammed from top to bottom with items both recognized and fantastical. A stew pot sat beside a glowing orb. A fan wrought of delicate silver filigree lay on a bolt of satin. A chest heaped with gold and jewels was topped by a handful of scroll cases. Even a single coin from that chest would buy food for a month if carefully managed.

As if reading his mind, Velachaz reached into the chest and scooped up a handful of the glittering coins. He spilled them into Teman's hand. "These are for you."

The boy stared down at the ten bright disks. It was more fortune than he ever had dreamed of. He looked up at the wizard with a puzzled frown. "Why?"

"Because you need them...because I don't... because I too wished for something better when I was a boy." Velachaz hung his cloak on a peg. Without its concealing folds, Teman noticed for the first time how the wizard's right arm hung awkward and useless at his side.

Velachaz followed his eye. "Ahh...yes. The rumors do not mention that the fearsome Velachaz is only half a man, and we must be sure to keep it that way. Our little secret, yes? A bit of advice, my young friend— never fight a dragon alone—not even a baby one."

Without the sweeping cape, Teman's sharp eyes detected a slight hesitation to his companion's step as well. Despite the limp, the wizard moved swiftly around his home, and a fire soon crackled merrily on the hearth while steam spiraled up from a pair of bowls on the table. The heady scent of carrots and potatoes mixed with the savory smell of roast mutton, and Teman's head swam from hunger.

"Come and eat, boy." The wizard beamed, indicating a chair for Teman. "The food is plain, but satisfying. I think you'll find it to your taste—"

Suddenly, his smile wavered and faded into a frown. "What shall I call you, lad? I can't keep calling you 'boy'."

"M-my name is Teman."

"And you must call me Vela—all that terribly wicked business you can forget about. It is awfully tiresome trying to live up to such a reputation, and my friends know better." Velachaz winked at him.

Teman sat down at the table, and soon not a scrap of food remained in his bowl.

"You were hungry, weren't you, Teman?"

"Aye."

"You are awfully young to be on the streets alone, lad."

"My mother died last winter, and my father beat me for it. I-I know it was his grief that made him do it, but I thought it would be better for us both if I left. I hear he has a new family now. He doesn't need me anymore."

"Teman, he probably needs you more than you'll ever know. But, his loss is my gain. Because I need a strong, smart boy, with the heart of a lion—like you."

"But I am none of those things, sir."

"Oh, but you are. I watched those boys chase you through the streets for hours, and you had wit enough to keep ahead of them, though I know you were exhausted. I was tempted to intervene...but I knew you wouldn't thank me for it.

"You tried to slip away from me, but when I stopped you, you faced whatever consequences would come from my wrath with a brave heart and a lifted head. Oh, yes. You are an exceptional boy. I need a boy like you to be my right hand."

Velachaz rose to his feet and began to pace about the room, as if it pained him to sit still for any length of time. "I cannot let the world know of my physical weaknesses. It fears Magick far too much, and would seek to destroy me. I have hid it this long, but it is getting harder and harder to do as more of the townsfolk feel they have outgrown Magick and its mysteries."

He swung around to face Teman, his eyes alight with excitement. "But if you will stand always to my right, and do as I will teach you, we can trick the world into seeing what we wish it to see. In return, I will give you a warm bed, good food, and clean clothes... and I will train you in the lesser ways of Magick. What do you say, Teman—will you become the right hand of Velachaz?"

Teman thought of a home...food on the table... warm fire...companionship. It was a strange twist of fortune—from living on the streets to apprentice mage in one brief hour—but that didn't lessen its attractions. "I'd be honored, my lord Vela."

And so, his apprenticeship began.

CHAPTER 2

The Principles of Magic

Drifting up toward wakefulness, Teman remembered the night before with regret. It had been a beautiful dream. He could almost feel the warmth of the thick blanket covering him even now, and in his half-waking he reached out and touched soft wool. Breath caught between inhalation and release, he let his fingertips explore the fabric, not yet daring to open his eyes. There were tiny defects in the weave that argued against an imaginary origin—what dreamer includes the flaws—but he still remained unconvinced...until the heavenly scent of freshly baked bread and the sizzling pop of frying bacon assailed his other senses. Finally, his eyes cracked open, wary of full commitment even yet.

He found himself lying on a comfortable pallet beside a gently crackling fire. Levering himself up on one elbow, Teman sleepily rubbed away the last remnants of the night.

"Good morning," came a cheerful voice from the other side of the hearth. "I was beginning to think you would sleep the day away."

Teman instantly bounded to his feet, instinctively ducking the expected blow for his laziness. "I'm sorry! It won't happen again, Master Velachaz."

A frown creased Velachaz's forehead, and his voice took on the calm measured tone that Teman was already beginning to equate with Vela damping down his own emotions. "I wish I could give you back the childhood that has been stolen from you, my boy, but I can't. However, you must believe this—I will never beat you. I will try never to ask you to do anything I don't think you are ready for...though this I can't promise. But most importantly, I will never punish you for being a child, and children need sleep...or so I've been told. I must confess, I have forgotten much of what it is like to be a child. You must help me remember. Now, if that is settled, come and eat, Tay. Today you begin your education."

Teman felt a little thrill of happiness inside. That was the second time Vela had called him "Tay." No one had given him a nickname of his own before. It made him feel special.

Obediently, he slid into the offered chair, noticing as he did so that Velachaz's face remained thoughtful. The wizard's hand half-lifted as if to reach out...but the moment passed, and Vela conjured forth his dazzling smile again. "I hope you like your bacon a bit well-done," the magic-user continued. "Cooking is not one of my better skills. You don't happen to be good at it, do you...?"

Teman shook his head shyly, and Velachaz shrugged. "Oh well, we'll just have to make do." He placed a plate before the boy, and then busied himself with other things, giving Teman much appreciated privacy to eat.

The new apprentice examined his surroundings in greater detail as he wolfed down the meal. Sunlight streamed into the room from windows high above the floor. By its less forgiving beams, the fine furnishings and exotic fixtures became a little rough around the edges—here a table leg propped up by a thick book, there a threadbare spot in the intricate pattern of the rug—but the chest of gold remained, and the aura of magic that filled the room was even more intense, if possible. It tingled up his spine like little dancing lightning bolts, and he felt like giggling as it tickled his senses.

"It makes me feel like laughing a thousand times a day," Vela murmured, startling Teman out of his daydream.

"How did you...?"

Vela chuckled. "Like calls to like, you know. I see so much of myself in your eyes. Now—are you ready to go to work?"

Teman nodded cautiously, and Vela's beautiful laugh rang out. "Don't look so terrified, little mouse. I think you will enjoy this." Vela limped to the table, awkwardly balancing a copper bowl filled with water. He set it down in front of the boy and stepped back. "Now, I want you to stare into this basin. Focus your thoughts on a particular event that you remember well. Something that made you happy."

The boy shrugged, and looked at the liquid in the bowl. "What am I supposed to do?"

"You must concentrate," Vela repeated. "If what I suspect is true, you will see your heart's desire." The mage rested his hand on Teman's shoulder for a moment. "I will leave you to your visions."

Teman stared intently into the copper basin of water. Vela had promised if he concentrated hard enough, the magic would come...but all he saw was himself staring back. The sight distracted him, and he took stock of the picture.

His features were thin and rather pinched, but the bone structure was finely chiseled and would someday yield a handsome man. His hair was badly in need of cutting—an indifferent brown in color, with reddish highlights when the sun caught it newly washed. His eyes were a greenish-gold that deepened to twilight moss when his mood was dark, and danced with a sunlight twinkle when he was happy. When his smile broke through, it was a charming, crooked grin more contagious than wildfire. All in all, it was not a bad face. He could see echoes of his mother in it...

With a sudden gasp, he realized it was his mother he saw. The magic had broken through. Before dazzled eyes, the last time he had seen his mother happy—before her wasting illness—replayed within the liquid mirror. They walked the streets of last fall's Hay Market Faire. She had been so beautiful, her laughter ringing merrily as they watched a troupe of acrobats clowning for the crowd. His eyes filled with tears as he remembered how her love had warmed his childhood. The tears spilled over to run down his cheek and drop into the bowl. The spell was broken, and the liquid just water once more. He swallowed hard, struggling to regain control.

"I'm sorry, mouse," came a soft voice behind him. "I didn't mean to cause you pain."

"No...it's all right. It was a wondrous thing."

"So, my boy! Are you ready for your first lesson?"

"As you wish, Master Vela." Teman rose to his feet, unsure what to expect.

Velachaz laughed heartily. "I'm not going to eat you, lad! Come, put this on. There is a chill to the air this morning." The wizard tossed him a heavy woolen cape of deep forest green.

Teman caught the cape and clasped it over his shoulder. It was the finest garment he'd ever worn, and he secretly stroked the soft fabric.

"It is a gift, boy. I can't have you freezing to death on me."

"Th-thank you, sir," Teman stammered in wonder.

"Come." Vela threw his own cloak about his shoulders and drew the hood up to hide his face. He opened the door for Teman, and waved him through it. "Let us begin!"

The next few hours passed like the wind. Vela showed Teman how to uncover the secret door to their rooms with a gesture and a spoken command—a small magic, but it thrilled the boy to know he held such power in his hand.

Then, Vela moved on to harnessing and channeling the magic. It was a tricky business, and Teman could not seem to get the commands correct.

"Better. Try it one more time—"

Teman's head fell back on his shoulders, and he groaned his protest to the indifferent sky. They had been at it all morning. He thought he was being fairly obvious about his feelings.

Vela didn't seem to notice. The magic-user stood against the wall of the stable, tapping his foot impatiently. "Come, now—again."

Teman gave up, pulled his thoughts around him like a cloak and concentrated on focusing his will. He pictured the desired result in his head, took a deep breath, and uttered the words Velachaz had taught him. They were nonsense to him—jumbles of sound that held no meaning—but the wizard had explained that the language of magic was unlike their own.

This time, as he spoke the incantation, the strange tingling he had briefly sensed earlier began to radiate outward from the very center of his being. The tickling sensation grew stronger as he recited the words, until—as he finished the command—he actually felt the power flow down his arm and shoot in a directed burst from his fingertips. Teman felt as if an enormous hand shoved him none too gently in the center of the chest, and the next thing he knew, he was lying on his back with a fearsome ache where his head had contacted the hard straw-covered ground behind the stables. He groaned.

Vela was instantly at his side, awkwardly helping him to sit up. "Are you all right, lad? That shouldn't have happened."

He looked to the magic-user for an explanation and swallowed his protest at the sight of Vela's face. It wore an expression of bewilderment that might have been amusing under other circumstances, but—after what had just happened—was instead rather alarming.

"What did happen?" he asked timidly. "Didn't I do it right?"

"Oh, you did it perfectly. Too perfectly, in fact. It was a simple spell. Those hand signals I taught you must be done while the incantation is being spoken—ideally, with the right hand. I did not expect that backlash of energy. Are you sure neither of your parents knew any Magic?"

"Not that I know of."

"The only way the spell could have had any effect upon you is if you have True Magic...the kind that can't be taught. Come here, boy." Vela had Teman lean up against the stable wall, staring intently at his new apprentice. "You must be a Natural..."

The intensity of Vela's gaze was rather alarming, and Teman shifted restlessly, ready to make a dash for it if necessary. With his usual uncanny perception, Vela seemed to read his thoughts. "Don't worry, Tay—I promise I won't bite."

The boy felt his cheeks grow hot, and he squared his shoulders. "I'm not afraid anymore, Master Vela."

"Yes, you are—or if you're not, you should be. Magic is always a dangerous game to play—but in the hands of an untrained Natural..." He shuddered, leaving the sentence unfinished.

Teman gulped. "That's the second time you've said that...a natural. Natural what?"

Vela laughed his glorious laugh. "Don't look so green, little mouse! Now that I know your potential, you shan't remain untrained for long. Show me your hands."

Obediently, Teman held out his hands, scowling when he saw how dirty they were, and how broken his nails. But the fingers themselves were long and slender, and his hands were well-formed and strong.

Vela examined them critically. "You must begin to take better care, mouse. Your hands will become your livelihood—and mine. Fortune surely smiled on me when She sent you to be my right arm.

"You see, my boy, there are basically three types of people in this world as regards Magic—"

Teman had noticed before that when Velachaz spoke the word "magic," one could hear that it was a name rather than an abstract concept. As if Magic were itself a great beast that could be played with, and harnessed, but never fully tamed. "I don't understand, Master Vela."

"It's like this. The vast majority of people in the world are ignored by Magic all their lives. Oh, you can use Magic against them, or for them, but never through them.

"The second type of people—a vastly smaller number—can be taught the basics of Magic—simple spells like building a fire, or making flowers grow taller—after much practice and a great deal of difficulty. They can work these small spells, but it will always be a chore for them—exhausting at best, and quite possibly dangerous.

"But the third...Ah, the third type of person is both lucky and cursed. They are the bare handful of us to whom Magic is as natural as breathing...those of us who channel Her power and bend it to our own devices. To us, the Art is no chore, but a necessity. The use of Magic the only way to feel truly alive.

"A very good student of the second type can rise to be a competent wizard—but even the least-trained Natural can best him in a duel, because the Magic will come to his aid. You have the Gift, lad."

Teman ducked his head at the praise. He was unused to kind words, being more often graced with a good swift kick.

Vela patted the boy's shoulder fondly. "I have some matters to attend to that require I work alone. Keep practicing, and be home for dinner."

Home...the word sent a thrill through Teman that made him shiver. "Aye, Master."

He watched Vela limp toward their rooms and felt his heart swell with emotion. Home.

Left to his own devices, and ordered not to return to the house for a while, Teman wandered to the outskirts of town looking for a more private place to practice his new skills. The sooner he could control his gift, the sooner Vela would really be able to use his services. He didn't know why it was so important to him that the magic-user be able to rely on him, but it was. Perhaps it was because he'd never felt needed before. Loved, yes—but not needed. In fact, usually just the opposite. Even his doting mother had often asked him to get out from underfoot so she might do her own work.

Teman found a large, flat field just south of town. There was no livestock grazing in the pasture, and it was late enough in the day that there were no children playing in the tall grass, as there probably had been earlier.

Teman made one more exploration of the field to make sure that he was alone, and then sank down tailor-fashion onto the ground. Closing his eyes, he concentrated as Vela had taught him, mentally gathering all his will into a little ball in the pit of his stomach.

Keeping his eyes closed so he wouldn't be distracted, he slowly rose to his feet. He took a deep breath and sent forth the energy with the words of the spell, letting it flow out his outstretched fingertips.

Two things happened at once—Teman felt the magic fly, and he heard a startled exclamation from in front of him. His eyes sprang open, darting about for the source of the cry. A few yards distant, a young man lay sprawled upon his back. A huge black horse thundered away in the opposite direction, as fast as its legs would carry him.

CHAPTER 3

"Gaily Bedight a Gallant Knight..."

"Oh, no!" Teman gulped, running toward the prone figure. "Please don't let him be dead!" he prayed to Whomever might be listening.

Arriving at the young man's side, Teman helped the stranger to his feet. "Are you all right?" he cried anxiously, attention split between the man and scanning the meadow for the runaway horse.

"I'm okay," the newcomer shrugged, dusting himself off. "This happens all the time." He put two fingers in his mouth and gave a shrill whistle. The big black horse trotted up to him like a puppy.

"You've gone and scared our new friend, Ducky," he scolded, patting the stallion's velvety muzzle. "That's no way to start an acquaintance."

Teman stared at the stranger.

This has got to be the oddest human being I've ever met.

When he studied the man more closely, he realized his initial impression had been misleading. Although the stranger towered above him, he was probably no more than five or six years older than Teman himself.

"My name is Galen," grinned the youth, thrusting out a muddy hand. "This is Ducky. His name was originally 'The Grand Duke Caliban,' but that sounded so formal. He seems to like Ducky better."

The big stallion whinnied and tossed his head—for all the world as if he were agreeing. Galen laughed merrily, his pleasure contagious. Teman found himself grinning along with the curious stranger.

"I'm sorry, I didn't catch your name," Galen said politely. Teman realized with a start that he hadn't offered it.

"Oh, I'm sorry. My name is Teman, but my friends call me Tay," he replied, shaking the proffered hand. His heart swelled merely to offer the new name. "Let me at least offer you a meal and a place to wash up."

"I never turn down food," acknowledged Galen cheerfully. "It's not easy being on a quest, you know. There are no servants calling you to dinner, or picking up after you..."

"You are on a quest?" Tay fell into step beside the older boy as they headed into town.

"Oh, yes. A most noble quest. I seek to slay a dragon and remove a dread curse."

"A curse?"

"Aye." Galen picked himself up from the ground, where he had fallen after tripping over a tree root. It was the only tree in the meadow—and the only root protruding above the ground. "I am a knight, you see—or I will be, if I slay this dragon before my eighteenth birthday."

"And how long does that give you to fulfill this quest?"

"Three months. But the problem is, I'm rather lost, you see..."

"Perhaps my master can be of service. He is a very wise and powerful wizard."

"Not the terribly wicked Velachaz!" cried Galen, backing away dramatically and sitting hard as he entangled his sword between his feet.

Tay shook his head and reached out to help Galen stand. "Don't believe everything you hear! Vela is the kindest man I know!"

"Well, truth be told—I can use all the help I can get. It's this curse, you see."

"Just what exactly is the curse?"

Galen sighed. "Oh, a most grievous one. If I do not slay the dragon before my coming-of-age at eighteen, my life will come to a swift and terrible end. So my mother tells me."

"It seems to me much more likely you will fulfill that prophecy if you do face the dragon."

"You may be right," admitted Galen. Then he continued philosophically, "Still...it would be a glorious battle. How many men have faced a dragon and lived to tell about it?"

"My master Vela has."

"Really? Was it a fight to the death?"

"Very nearly—his. And the dragon he faced was a mere hatchling. Don't you see how foolish your quest may be?"

Galen stopped dead in his tracks and drew himself up to his full height. "Never tell a hero that his quest is a foolish one. No matter how it may seem to you, his honor is at stake. I may have little else, but I have my honor."

The stallion butted him in the small of the back, breaking his grand pose. "Oh—and Ducky. I do have Ducky."

"Well, think of Ducky, then. What will he do without you? What will the dragon do with him? I don't think you've planned this whole thing out very thoroughly."

"Of course not! I am a man of action!" Galen whipped out his sword with a grand flourish that nearly took off Tay's ear.

The smaller boy ducked just in time, and carefully stepped a little further away from his companion. They made it to the outskirts of town without further incident, but Teman watched in wonder as the young knight stared about him with slack-jawed amazement. "What a noble city!" he shouted, spinning in a circle, arms wide as if to embrace the whole of it.

Teman skipped back to avoid being hit. "Where do you come from that Farlea seems a city?"

"My castle—well, it's more like a keep, actually—is many leagues away, near the sea. My mother and father already had six sons before I was born. I began my arrival into this world on the last night of one century and finished in the next. At first my mother thought that was an extremely lucky sign. Until a fortune-teller told her it was actually an evil omen—especially with a seventh son—but she took it fairly well. Of course, my next youngest brother is twice my age, and the family had pretty much decided on inheritances and so forth before I was born." Galen flicked idly at stray wisps of grass with the tip of his sword. "I rather threw everything a-kilter...until the curse came along."

A sneaking suspicion began to tickle the back of Teman's mind, but he kept it to himself. They walked in silence for a time, each wrapped up in his own little world.

Tay glanced around him as Galen took in the sights of the city. He tried to imagine seeing the filthy streets for the first time, but they remained narrow and dirty to him—the slums were still slums.

They arrived at the hidden doorway to Vela's apartments, and Galen absentmindedly reached forward to knock before turning to Teman. "Oh...I guess we don't need to bother knocking if you are apprenticed here."

It was Tay's turn to stare. He looked at the wall where he knew the doorway to be, but the spell was still in place. Without the secret pass of the hand and the whispered incantation that Velachaz had taught him, the doorway was invisible to the naked eye—yet Galen's hand hovered unerringly over the very center of the panel, ready to rap upon it.

Tay quickly dispelled the glamour on the door and led the way into the house. "Master!" he called. "We have a visitor requiring your assistance."

Vela appeared at the head of the stairway to the loft where his private study lay. A whip-crack of thunder split the still room, and a bolt of lightning arced to light the logs laid in the fireplace. The wizard's presence seemed to fill the room as he glowered down at the boys. "Who dares disturb the terribly wicked—Galen! What in thunder are you doing here, boy?" With a delighted whoop, Vela fairly flew across the room and swept Galen into the circle of his good arm.

Galen returned the bear hug with enthusiasm. "Uncle Vela! It is good to see you again."

"Uncle..." A wave of confusion hit Teman as he tried to make sense of this new turn of events.

Vela's laughter rang against the rafters. "What have you been telling this poor lad, you rascal?"

"Nothing but truth...but not all of that, perhaps." Galen grinned in reply. "I'm sorry to have teased you so, Teman, but it was delightful fun."

"I don't understand."

"Vela is my mother's brother," explained Galen, removing his sword belt and tossing the blade aside. "A terribly wicked fraud is what he is. 'The kindest man I know,' I believe you said?"

Tay felt his cheeks grow hot, but he bit back the angry remark that sprang to his lips. He was working hard at curbing his temper, and knew that there had been no harm meant, but it hurt him to be treated like a child just when he had begun to feel grown up.

"Don't tease the boy, Galen. He is more use to me than you have ever been. What brings you here, nephew?"

"It is time to slay the dragon," Galen cried, posing heroically. "Umm…you don't happen to know where it lives, do you?"

Teman shook his head. He had a feeling this was going to be a long quest.

Dinner was a happy affair that evening. Galen had them both laughing merrily as he shared stories of his misadventures while he journeyed in search of the dragon.

"But why do you think that the only way to end the curse is to slay the dragon?" Teman asked Galen curiously. "What exactly did your mother say?"

"Well, oddly enough, every time I ask her about it she moans, says my life will come to a swift and terrible end, and starts to cry. I finally quit asking and just accepted that the dragon was a part of it."

Vela massaged his crippled shoulder absentmindedly. "Dragons are nothing to trifle with, nephew. Perhaps you had better just settle here with us and leave the quest be."

Galen shook his head regretfully. "It is a tempting offer, Uncle Vela, but it is no longer up to me. You see, there is another wrinkle to the problem now. The king has heard about the quest, and since no one wants a dragon running around loose in his kingdom, he has decided my quest is as good an opportunity as any to get rid of the creature. He told Father if I slay the dragon, he will give me my knighthood and a small holding of my own so there will be no need to worry about me sharing the estate. The brothers were all very glad to hear it. However, if I don't slay the dragon, then he will take all of Father's lands to pay for the damage the dragon has already done, and the boys will get nothing."

"Well, what if the dragon kills you instead?" Tay asked.

"If I were to die in battle then the king has promised that he will reward my brave sacrifice by increasing Father's lands by six hundred acres—another hundred acres apiece for each of my brothers—"

All of Teman's earlier suspicions were confirmed. This quest was merely a way to get rid of an unwanted son.

"I know what you're thinking," Galen murmured, and Teman jumped, hoping that it wasn't true. "I know that I haven't got much chance against the beast, but what have I got to lose?"

"Your life?" Vela rose to his feet and limped to lean against the mantle, staring into the fire. Tay could see the anger in the mage's face that he struggled to control. "I will come with you, Galen," Vela muttered. "No one should have to fight such a battle alone. It would be suicide."

"With you on my side, I know we will slay the monster!" Galen rose to his feet with a sweeping gesture, and knocked his water goblet to the floor with a clatter, spilling liquid across the stones in a splashing arc.

Teman sighed and went to fetch a towel.

"You can sleep here by the fire with Teman tonight," Vela told Galen, "and tomorrow we will decide how best to proceed."

"I am rather tired." Galen nodded, stifling a yawn. "Questing is hard work."

Teman spread a pallet for the knight opposite his own, and the youth sank down upon the blankets gratefully. "This feels wonderful... That's another thing I hate about questing—the hard beds, or maybe I should say lack of them. I'm tired of sleeping on rocks."

"I really don't think you're cut out to be a knight," Teman said softly.

"I know. If it weren't for the king, I'd be perfectly happy with a little farm somewhere, but I have no right to ruin my brothers for my own selfishness."

"So you'll die against the dragon?"

"Oh, I don't know," replied Galen, lying back, with his fingers laced behind his head. "I just might win. There's always hope."

Teman felt a surge of pity for the other's foolish hope, and a fierce admiration for his incredible courage. It was long after Galen's even breathing told that he slept before Tay's eyes closed, and his dreams were filled with sharp teeth and slashing claws.

CHAPTER 4

The Quest Begins

When Tay awoke the next morning, the terror that had invaded his dreams still clung uneasily to the corners of his imagination, but there was no doubt in his mind that he would follow Velachaz and Galen on the quest. Not only was it an adventure such as most boys merely dreamed about, it was also a chance to prove to Vela that he could be the helper the wizard needed him to be.

Dragging a hand across sleepy eyes, he sat up and looked around. Galen was still asleep, curled like a kitten on the other side of the hearth. Vela stood in the open doorway, staring out into the dawn. As Tay moved, the mage turned to him, smiling crookedly.

"Good morning," Vela murmured softly. "I didn't mean to wake you."

Tay gathered his bedding neatly and stowed it away. "You didn't, Master. I was dreaming—"

"Of dragons?"

"Yes." Tay crossed the stone floor to stand beside Vela. It was cold beneath his bare feet. "Do you really think he can defeat this beast?"

Vela shrugged slightly. "I don't know. I doubt it. But I don't plan to let him face it alone—or be slain just so his brothers don't have to give him his share of the inheritance." Vela's jaw tightened in anger. "He is the only one of the seven with even a spark of humor or imagination, and the others don't know what to make of him. But that's no excuse for sending him to his death."

Tay didn't know what he could say that would comfort, so he didn't try. Sometimes it is more important just to listen.

Vela patted the boy's shoulder absentmindedly and limped toward the stairway leading to his loft. He walked more slowly today, pausing now and then to shift his weight from his bad leg, as if it pained him more than usual this morning.

Tay frowned. Was it the reminder of dragons that deepened the ache? Quietly, he began to move around the kitchen, putting together breakfast so that Vela wouldn't have to. By the time he had it ready, Galen was awake, stretching and yawning hugely.

Tay called up to Vela in the study, handing the mage a steaming mug of tea as he came downstairs.

"Thank you, my boy." Vela nodded, accepting it gratefully. "So, Galen. Tell me all you know about dragons."

"Well," Galen settled himself on a bench tailor-fashion with his own cup of tea, "they are very big, very vicious, though not overly bright, and they breathe fire—"

"Wrong, wrong, and wrong!" Vela thundered, sitting across from his nephew and fixing him with a piercing stare. "Not all dragons are large. They vary in size from those that could sit on the palm of your hand to those the height of the trees. Though dragons can be—and often are—quite cruel, they are also wickedly cunning, and likely could get the better of an innocent like you even on a bad day. And not all dragons breath fire—some have breath as cold as ice, while others spit lightning. Never assume you know a dragon's strengths and weaknesses from the gossip you hear. The only way to really know the truth about a particular beast is to speak to it yourself."

"Speak to it? Do dragons talk?" cried Tay in wonder, forgetting in his excitement that he had meant only to listen.

"Indeed they do, lad," Vela replied, "though one should never trust what they say without some kind of proof."

"But, if they are intelligent," Tay frowned, "why don't you just ask the creature to leave the king's lands alone?"

Galen exploded with laughter. "That's the silliest thing I've ever heard!"

Teman felt the heat rush to his cheeks, and he ducked his head. Vela laid a hand on his shoulder. "Galen, you are a fool. This boy has a great deal more sense than you do. He has hit upon the only possible solution which would save you from being torn apart and still fulfill the king's order—unless you want to throw your life away..."

"Of course not," Galen protested. "But—talk to the dragon?"

"Would you rather kill it?"

"No...not really...I don't even like to squash bugs."

"Then I suggest you start thinking about what you want to say." Vela patted Tay's shoulder. "I'll start packing."

After a hectic flurry of preparation, the three adventurers stood at last in the stables. Vela leaned against the wall of Ducky's stall as Galen saddled the big black horse, talking excitedly to the animal, which nodded his great head as if understanding every word. Tay bit his lip nervously then tugged on Vela's sleeve.

The mage bent to listen.

"Master Vela," whispered Teman miserably, "I don't know how to ride."

"Hmm, I see. That could be a problem."

Ducky's ears swiveled toward them, and he gently butted Galen in the chest with his great velvety nose. Galen turned to Teman. "You can ride with me on Ducky, if you like. He's quite sure-footed, and he will be very careful." Ducky's head swung up and down in a definite nod.

Tay stepped up to the stallion and tentatively stroked his soft muzzle, looking deep into the big brown eyes that stared intelligently back at him. He smiled at the horse and murmured softly, "Thank you. I would like that."

"It's settled then." Vela limped to the stall of a delicate gray mare with a white star on her forehead, and spoke to her softly as he placed a worn saddle on her back. They were obviously old friends.

Galen helped Tay to mount onto Ducky's broad back then led the horse out into the sunlight. Vela followed on the mare, leading a second packhorse. Once they were clear of the stables, Galen leapt lightly into the saddle and cried happily, "We're off!" He kicked Ducky into motion, and they began their journey.

It didn't take Tay long to get over his nervousness, because the stallion had a smooth gait, and an uncanny way of choosing the best footing on the path. Before they had gotten far, Galen spun around in the saddle to lean against the high saddle horn and face Tay as they rode.

The apprentice frowned. "Don't you need to watch where we're going?"

"Not really." Galen shrugged. "Ducky will take care of us." The older boy began to tell Tay more of his previous adventures on the quest, illustrating them with broad sweeping gestures that seemed sure to fling him from his precarious perch, but he kept his seat, and the morning passed swiftly. Vela rode in silence, apparently lost in thought, and every now and then, Tay felt a twinge of guilt that he was enjoying himself so much when the quest could so easily end in disaster.

After a lunch eaten under the branches of a huge spreading oak tree, Velachaz resumed Tay's training while Galen napped, his head resting on a protruding root. Today Vela showed the boy how to call forth a breeze. Teman's efforts barely ruffled the tree leaves, but it was still enough to make his heart sing inside him.

When they started on their way soon afterward, Tay felt confident enough to perch amongst the baggage on the ancient sorrel packhorse rather than make Ducky carry double. He continued to practice his new spell, calling miniature whirlwinds to dance on either side of the road.

Galen rode a little ahead of the others now, singing softly to himself in a beautiful, unexpectedly deep baritone. A dragonfly lit on the young knight's shoulder, and Tay whispered the words of the wind spell to blow it away.

Nothing happened.

Puzzled by the failure, Tay concentrated on focusing the magic and tried again. Ducky's tail blew in the breeze, and the gilt bells on his harness tinkled faintly, but not a hair on Galen's head so much as stirred. The dragonfly, apparently rested, buzzed off of its own accord.

Tay turned toward Vela in bewilderment to find the wizard watching him with a broad grin on his handsome face. Tay frowned. There was no need to take pleasure in his failure.

Vela raised a finger to his lips and pulled back on his reins, halting the mare. He gestured Tay to his side, and the boy awkwardly maneuvered the sorrel to stand beside the gray.

"What happened?" he asked softly. "What did I do wrong?"

"No, no, my boy—you did nothing wrong. You performed the spell beautifully."

"Then why didn't it work?"

Velachaz gave a rueful chuckle. "Tay, my lad, when I spoke of the three categories of people in this world with regards to Magic, I neglected to mention the fourth type...so rare that you will meet perhaps one in your lifetime. These are the few souls Magic utterly refuses to have any truck with at all. I had forgotten that Galen was one of that breed."

"What does that mean?"

"No charm can aid them—and no curse harm them. Which does seem to throw doubt on his present danger, now doesn't it? You cannot hurt them with spells, but neither can you help. Magic rolls away from them like water from a duck's back. And because they miss the little evidences of Magic, it is harder for them to believe in the whole. That is why Galen is so fearless going against the dragon—he doesn't fully believe in its power, you see—and therefore he can't truly be frightened of it. This could be a serious problem when we do find the creature's lair. I do wish I'd remembered Galen was one of these ducks."

Tay did not find this news particularly encouraging. "But if he isn't cursed, then what about—?"

"More likely more of his sheer inherent clumsiness. He is a good-hearted fellow, is Galen, but he is also the most accident-prone human being I've ever met!"

With a thoughtful frown, Vela urged the mare up beside Ducky and began to argue softly with Galen. Tay couldn't hear the words, but since he hadn't been included in the discussion, he had a feeling he wasn't supposed to hear. With a twinge of jealousy he pulled the sorrel's reins, falling further behind and feeling just a little sorry for himself.

There was a gentle whir of wings beside his ear, and he brushed at it absentmindedly.

"Hey! Watch out!" squeaked an indignant little voice, and Teman jerked around, almost throwing himself off the horse. Hovering in mid-air was a tiny creature with the iridescent wings of a dragonfly. "You nearly blew me away before, and now you try to swat me out of the air! What kind of person are you?"

Tay could only stare. He had never seen anything like the creature before. It looked like a miniature version of the lizards he sometimes glimpsed sunning on the stable wall, but its eyes sparkled with intelligence, and its wings were dazzling shimmers as they beat to keep it hovering. "What are you?" the boy breathed in awe.

"What's the matter? Haven't you ever seen a dragonfly before?"

"Not like you."

"Perhaps you simply didn't look at it correctly."

"Where did you come from?"

"That's a rather personal question, isn't it? I don't ask you where you got those ridiculously long legs, or why you have no wings."

"I just meant where did you come from now."

"Oh, that's different then. I was passing by, and you looked like you could use some company."

Tay found it hard to believe the little creature's story, but it was fun to talk to, so he didn't say anything. "We are on a quest. To slay—to visit a dragon," he amended hastily, not knowing if there might be a family connection.

"Well, then! It's a good thing I came along. I know all about dragons." The little creature landed smoothly on Tay's shoulder, curling its tail around his neck and tucking its front feet beneath it like a cat.

"My name is Teman," the boy offered shyly, "but my friends call me Tay." The nickname still gave him a rush of pride. "What shall I call you?"

The creature tilted its head, as if giving the matter serious thought. "You may call me...Dart. Yes, I like that. Dart."

Teman grinned happily at the thought that he had something magical of his own to share with Velachaz, but the wizard was deep in conversation with Galen, so the boy didn't disturb his master just now. Instead, he was content to follow along behind, playing I Spy with Dart until the shadows began to lengthen, and the road become hard to see in the gathering twilight.

Reluctant to intrude, Tay concentrated his focus, and sent a breath of wind to tease at Vela's cloak. The wizard looked around at the tug of the breeze and gave an exclamation of surprise. "Why, look Galen! It will be nightfall soon. Unless you want to sleep under the stars again tonight, I suggest we find shelter."

Galen cast an uneasy glance at the sunset, which was fiery red bordered with a billowy bank of black clouds. "I doubt there will be stars tonight. It looks like we're in for rain before morning, and there is nothing worse than sleeping in wet clothes. We should be nearing a hamlet I've been through before. The inn isn't first-rate, but they have beds to offer, and a fine kitchen—when the cook's not drunk."

"Lead the way," Vela agreed with a nod.

Teman stole a peek at Dart, who was asleep on his shoulder, muzzle tucked between tiny paws. He debated whether this was a good time to tell Velachaz about his new companion, but decided to keep the secret to himself for a little while longer. After all, it was the first time he had ever had a secret all his own before...and such a special one at that!

He turned his attention back to keeping the packhorse from stumbling on the hard-to-see path. Galen soon led them into the yard of a rundown inn of silvery wood with a straw thatched roof and a ramshackle stable attached. Ducky stood contentedly munching on the overhanging edge of the thatch as Galen slid from the saddle and pushed open the door of the inn. The young knight turned back to the others before entering. "You had better wait for me here, until I'm sure they have rooms. This place can get a bit rough."

Vela raised an amused eyebrow, but dipped his head in acknowledgment.

Teman eased the sorrel up beside him. "Do you really think it could be dangerous?" the boy whispered nervously.

"Nothing my reputation can't handle," the wizard replied, "but it won't do to bruise the lad's ego. He is the hero of this quest, after all."

Tay shivered. It was easy to forget about Vela's reputation when they were alone together, but to the rest of the world the wizard was still the "terribly wicked," and there had to be some truth to the title.

"Don't look so green, mouse. I will behave." Vela grinned. "Unless, of course, they ask for trouble."

"How can you even joke about it, Master? The whole world fears your very name—"

"And if they weren't afraid of me, Teman, they might look too closely at the real man. I'm not happy that Fate has forced me into this role, but I would rather be feared than persecuted. The world is all too happy to fall upon the weak and helpless."

"But you're not helpless, even if..." Tay trailed off, unable to think of a way to say what was on his mind without causing Vela pain.

"Even if I am a cripple? Maybe not, but I am tired, and not in the mood to prove it today. Come, let's get the horses taken care of."

"What about Galen?"

"He'll find a room, or if not, we can sleep in the stable. It makes no difference to me."

Teman felt a soft scrabbling movement on his shoulder, and jumped, reaching automatically to brush at it before he remembered Dart. He stopped his hand just in time, but the gesture drew Vela's eye.

"Hello," breathed the wizard, "what have we here?" He leaned over from the mare and held out his ringed finger.

Dart cocked his head and looked into the mage's face. Then he stepped off of Tay's shoulder and onto Vela's finger.

Vela lifted his hand to get a better look at the little creature. "Where did you come from?" he murmured with a soft laugh.

Dart rose on his back legs, folding his forelegs across his chest indignantly. "Why does everyone keep asking me that question? Is it really your business?"

The courtyard rang with Vela's delighted laughter, and Tay found himself grinning along. The little flyer huffed and tossed its head, then flew back to Tay's shoulder, seeking shelter behind his neck as if it were a large tree trunk. "He came to me this afternoon," Tay explained, trying in vain to untangle Dart from his hair. "May he come with us?"

"Well, I would say that was entirely up to him," Vela answered, "but he is welcome as far as I am concerned." He bowed to the little dragonfly from his saddle. "Now, come. Let us get these animals something to eat. They've worked hard today."

Teman nodded, slipping to the ground and helping Vela dismount. He took up Ducky's reins as well as his own, and followed Velachaz into the stable.

When they joined Galen inside the inn, Tay had Dart safely hidden in the folds of his cloak. The boy looked around the rough common room with interest. This was the first journey he had ever taken beyond the edges of Farlea, and everything was spiced with adventure. Even the dirty, rundown building seemed like a palace to his dazzled eyes. Suddenly it was easier to understand Galen's delight in Farlea.

Galen stood beside the bar, swapping stories with the innkeeper as they drank from pewter mugs. Vela frowned at his nephew, and Galen laughed. "Don't worry, Uncle. There is nothing harder than cider in my cup. Would you like a pint?"

"Indeed. It has been a dry day." Vela sat wearily at a table near the bar, and Teman noticed lines of pain bracketing the wizard's mouth. The mage winced as he straightened his right leg under the table, massaging his knee with his good hand.

Tay bit his lip and tried to think of anything he could do to help. He wished he knew more about Magic! The thought made him smile. He realized that he was beginning to think of it in capital letters too.

Galen brought over mugs of cider for his companions. Tay sat down with the others. The cider was sweet and cold, and it banished the thirst he had picked up on the long ride. Already Teman could feel his muscles tightening up after the unaccustomed exercise, and he could imagine the discomfort Vela must feel.

As he drained the last of his cider a girl stepped up to their table. She was dressed in a shapeless worn gown that hung awkwardly on her bony shoulders, and the apron wrapped around her thin waist circled her twice. But she had friendly brown eyes, and a shy smile brushed her lips as she asked if they would like something to eat. Tay guessed that she was a little older than he was, and a little younger than Galen, but he couldn't tell for sure.

"Indeed we do, my lady," Galen answered heartily, propping elbows on the table. "What have you in your kitchen for three stout adventurers who go to slay a dragon?"

The girl tossed her head to throw a lock of hair the color of fresh honey out of her eyes, and looked doubtfully at the young knight. "Do you know any such, sir?"

"Why, we ourselves, my girl! We go even now to chase the monster to its lair." Galen seemed offended that she would doubt him.

"Forgive me, sir," the girl giggled, "but you don't look much like dragon-slayers."

Galen opened his mouth to protest, but Vela smoothly broke in, "You are right, my dear. Pay no attention to my nephew's foolishness. We are merely passing through on our way north."

The girl sighed. "Still, it must be fine to travel—"

"Sally, quit lagging about! You've got work to do!" roared a voice from the kitchen, and the girl jumped.

Vela smiled at her, and handed her two gold coins. "We will have three of the house's best dinners, and the second coin is for your own, Sally."

Her eyes widened at the gift, and she tucked the coin inside the belt of her apron, dropping an awkward curtsey. "I'll bring your meal, sir. As soon as I can, sir." Picking up the edge of her skirt where it dragged the ground, she scurried toward the kitchen.

Galen turned to Vela with a scowl. "Why didn't you want me to tell her the truth? I'm not ashamed of my quest."

"You needn't be. But you also needn't tell everyone you meet that you seek the dragon either. Many people have but to hear the name to panic. You may find yourself on the street because the innkeeper doesn't want to risk the dragon destroying his place, and can you blame him? If it were your home, would you want to call the creature's attention to it?"

"But the dragon is still leagues from here!" Galen scoffed.

"On horseback, perhaps. But dragons don't ride horses. They fly."

"Oh."

"It is not only the innkeeper you must be wary of either," Vela continued softly, leaning close to the young knight. "An adventurer who seeks to slay a dragon may have the experience of other quests behind him, and the treasure gained from them. There are several men in the corner over there who became very interested in you when you began your boasting."

Tay could not help glancing over at the table Vela indicated. There were five men seated around it, and any one of them looked like he could snap the slim young knight in two without a second thought. If the rough thugs decided Galen did indeed have riches worth stealing, Tay didn't know how he and his friends could possibly stop an attack. He gulped nervously.

Vela smiled at him. "Don't worry, mouse. You forget—I am the terribly wicked Velachaz." The smile grew cold, and Teman felt a shiver of fear run through him as—for just a moment—he saw the side of Vela that had earned him his reputation.

Sally returned with their dinners just then, giving Vela another of her shy smiles as she set the steaming bowls before them. The spicy aroma of mutton stew wafted up from the table, and the picnic under the tree suddenly seemed like days ago.

The food was delicious to appetites earned by a hard day's travel. Sally brought freshly baked bread to go with the stew, and the scent of the hot loaf brought a flash of memory, transporting Tay to his mother's kitchen...but this time the memory wasn't painful, merely sweet, and he smiled at the thought of her.

Soon however, in spite of a worried determination to stay awake all night in case Vela should need him, Tay found his head nodding forward as his eyes drifted shut of their own accord. It had been a long day, with more excitement—and exercise—than he was used to. Finally, he felt a gentle hand on his shoulder, and started awake to the sound of Vela's soft chuckle.

"Come, little mouse, we will have to fish you from your stew if we don't get you to bed."

"I'm all right," Tay protested. "Just let me splash my face with some cold water—"

Vela's face hardened into the no-nonsense expression Tay knew meant the wizard would not accept any argument. "You are exhausted, child, and you are no good to either one of us in this condition. Besides, Galen is yawning like a cavern, and I would really like the chance to rest myself." The stern mouth relaxed into a rueful grin. "After all, lad, this may be the last chance you ever get to sleep in a bed. You might as well take advantage of it."

The reminder of their mission was enough to convince Tay. They would need all their strength against the dragon. With a nod, he pushed away from the table to stand up. The twinge of pain from stiffened muscles made him gasp. He could barely force his legs to move as he followed Vela and Galen to their room.

Though he was so tired he could barely think Tay lay awake until long after the others were asleep. His imagination kept painting horrible pictures of slashing claws and flashing teeth behind his closed eyelids, forcing them open.

"What's the matter?" came a little voice at his shoulder, and Tay jerked up on one elbow, staring about him wildly. "Are you all right?"

Dart hovered beside him, shimmering wings a hazy blur in the moonlight. With the distraction of dinner, and the ache in every muscle, Teman had forgotten all about his newfound friend.

"I'm fine," he whispered back. "Just a little sore. I'd never ridden a horse before." Tay turned over to lie on his stomach, chin propped up on crossed arms as he watched the little creature flit about. "What about you? Are you hungry? I'm sorry I didn't think about your dinner."

"That's all right." Dart shrugged his wings, and came to rest on the edge of Tay's bed. "I found my own. Tay, are you really going to fight a dragon?"

Tay sighed. "Well, not me, exactly. Galen is the one who is supposed to fight it. I would rather talk to it, but Master Vela says there is no reasoning with them."

"Has he ever tried?"

"A dragon almost killed him."

"Before or after he tried to talk to it?"

Tay started to reply, and then realized he really didn't know.

Vela didn't really tell me much about the encounter, just that the creature was responsible for his injuries.

It obviously led to the wizard's mistrust of dragons, but could it all have been a horrible mistake?

"I'm not sure," he told Dart.

"Will you promise to talk to it before you let them kill it, Tay?"

"I can't promise, but I'll try." With the making of the pledge, Tay felt a weight lift from his heart, and he knew it was the right thing to do. "Thank you, Dart," he yawned, and by the time his head slid down onto the pillow of his arms, he was fast asleep.

CHAPTER 5

Ambushed!

It seemed he had barely closed his eyes before Teman was being shaken awake. The room was filled with gray dawn light, and the others were already dressed and packed. He tried to jump out of bed with his usual willingness, but the action made him cry out as taut muscles protested.

"Take it easy, lad," Vela soothed, laying a hand on the boy's shoulder and murmuring softly under his breath. When the wizard finished the spell, Tay felt the aches melt away like water running through a sieve.

"It can't keep the pain at bay forever, but you should ease the stiffness out by the time the Magic tires of you. Vela smiled. "Come, we must be on the road."

Galen tossed him a soft roll. "Here's breakfast."

Tay hurriedly gathered his things, munching on the roll as he packed. As he finished, Dart glided up and settled himself on Teman's shoulder. With his iridescent wings tucked across his back, almost invisible against the scarlet hide, he looked even more like a lizard instead of other dragonflies Tay had watched play at the creek. Dart twined his tail securely around Tay's neck and cocked his head alertly.

"You won't forget your promise?" he asked the boy.

"No...but don't mention it right now," Tay whispered, glancing uneasily at Vela as the wizard led the way toward the stable. "The others won't understand."

"But you will talk to it!" Dart squeaked anxiously.

"I said that I would do my best, and I will."

The little dragonfly sighed sadly, and put head on front paws, the picture of misery. Tay had a hard time not giggling, but he knew the creature was very upset and didn't want to be rude. He reached up tentatively and stroked the tiny head. "I promise," he breathed softly.

Dart nodded against his finger. "Thank you, Tay."

"Are you coming?" asked Vela from the stable doorway, a trace of impatience in his voice.

Tay ran to catch up.

As they journeyed, Tay felt the stiffness easing out of his muscles, and he found himself beginning to enjoy the ride. He amused himself by playing games with Dart and practicing his small Magics. They had not ridden far when they approached a stand of trees Velachaz told him was the beginning of the famous Parrot Wood.

Tay eyed the dark trees nervously. When he was a young child his mother had told him tales of the wicked men and strange creatures to be found beneath the trees of Parrot Wood. He was not particularly interested in meeting them.

Galen noticed his unease, and grinned. "Are you frightened of fairy stories, Tay?"

Tay felt his cheeks burn. Galen's teasing was starting to irritate him.

"There's no dishonor in sensible caution," Vela declared firmly, frowning at his nephew. "Just because you haven't the wits to be wary, that's no reason to scoff at the boy."

Galen's face flushed dull red in turn. "I'm sorry, Teman. I did not intend to be hurtful."

"That's all right," Tay replied diplomatically, "I shouldn't be nervous, with such a brave champion in our midst."

Galen straightened once more in his saddle, his spirits restored. "That's true," he nodded. The knight drew his sword with a flourish. Ducky snorted in protest as it swept past his ear. "I am here to protect you."

Before the last word of this gallant speech was fully out of Galen's mouth, a piercing whistle split the air, and they were set upon by a shouting band of rough-looking men brandishing clubs and pitchforks. Their mounts reared in fright, and Tay bit back his own panic, fighting to control the big packhorse as it tried to run away with him. He caught sight of Vela from the corner of his eye, as the mage struggled with the mare.

The wizard couldn't control the horse with his left hand and use it to cast a spell at the same time. The normally gentle mare was terrified, and she was bucking wildly, trying to shed herself of her burden so that she might flee the danger. Galen and Ducky were beset by a pair of the raiders, and the knight was flailing about him with his sword, unaware of his uncle's difficulty.

Without thinking, Teman recited the words of the wind spell, focusing all his concentration on the heavyset man who was reaching for the mare's bridle. Tay flung out his hand, and the huge scoundrel flew backward as if he had been pushed. The boy didn't stop to reflect on what he had done, but kicked the sorrel toward Vela's mare.

The wizard had managed to gain some measure of control over the frightened horse, but he still had his hand full trying to stop her from bolting. As Tay galloped closer, one of the attacking rogues dropped to the ground as if struck. Tay spun in the saddle, and stared open-mouthed at the spectacle that met his eye.

Standing half-hidden in the tall silvery grass of the plain, her skirts tucked up into the waistband of her apron, stood Sally, a sling whirling about her head as her eyes blazed with fury. Even as Tay watched, she let fly with a stone, and another of the men fell as if pole-axed. Galen cheered upon catching sight of their unexpected rescuer and slapped down one of his own attackers with the flat of his sword. When they found their quarry was not as helpless as they had expected, the remaining villains took to their heels and ran away.

Sally raced up to Vela, her bare feet flying across the grass. "My lord!" she cried anxiously. "Are you all right?"

Vela slumped forward to stroke the mare's sweaty neck and murmur soothingly to the high-strung animal, then turned his dazzling smile on Sally. "Thanks to you, my lady. We owe you a debt of gratitude."

Sally patted the mare's muzzle, shyly avoiding Vela's eye. "I heard them talking last night after you went up to sleep, my lord. They saw your gold and figured there would be more for the taking. I was afraid you wouldn't heed a warning, so I came out before you to help."

"I thank you again, my child," Vela replied gravely, then bent down in the saddle and lifted Sally's chin, capturing her gaze with his. "That was a very brave thing to do, Sally, but it was also very foolish. It will cause you trouble at home."

"I don't care! It was six against three. Besides, they only kept me in the kitchen because my mother worked there before she died. It wasn't really home."

Tay knew how she felt. It was worse than no shelter to live where you weren't wanted.

"Might I go with you, my lord?" Sally continued eagerly. "I can keep up and work my share."

"But you heard Galen say where we are bound, child."

"Then you really are going to slay a dragon?"

"Indeed we are," Galen interrupted. "A slip of a girl like you would only get in the way!"

Sally tossed her head angrily, throwing wayward bangs out of her eyes. "I didn't do so badly against those thieves, did I?"

"That was nothing compared to a dragon!" Galen jeered.

Vela looked over at Tay and asked solemnly, "What is your vote, my boy?"

Teman bit his lip thoughtfully. He studied Sally through his lashes. She was thin but wiry, and had proven that she was no giggling female like the village girls back home. He felt a strong kinship with the motherless kitchen wench. "I would be pleased to have Miss Sally join us," he said softly.

Sally smiled at him. Galen heaved a loud sigh of disapproval, jerking Ducky's head around and kicking him into a gallop away from the others.

"Master Vela—" Tay cried in alarm, making ready to follow the knight.

Vela shook his head. "Don't worry about Galen. He has a hot temper at times, but he will calm down and Ducky will bring him back safely. That horse has much more sense than its master."

Tay was surprised to hear the same thing he had thought to himself voiced aloud by Velachaz. He traced the knight's ride with his eye, half-listening as Vela formally invited Sally to join them.

"And now, I suppose you had better let Sally come up behind you on the packhorse, Teman. The mare is hard enough to control as it is, and by the time Galen comes to his senses, Ducky may be too tired to carry double."

Tay nodded, reaching down and helping Sally to mount behind him. She slipped her arms around his waist and confided softly, "I've never ridden on a horse before..."

Tay laughed. "Neither had I before yesterday. I suppose we'll learn together."

Sally suddenly gasped, "There's a lizard on your shoulder!" She reached up to brush the creature off, and Tay cried hastily, "No! It's all right. That's just Dart."

She pulled back from him. "What is it?"

"That's just my dragonfly."

"It's a lizard," she repeated, as if he were hard of hearing.

"That's what I thought too, at first. Dart!" Tay turned his head to look at the little animal and was rewarded by the attention of one sleepy black eye. "Dart, wake up! I want you to meet our new friend Sally."

Dart sat up on back legs, lazily stretching shimmering wings. He hooked his tail securely in Tay's collar, and turned to face the girl. "Pleased to meet you."

Sally laughed delightedly. "Isn't he marvelous!"

Dart preened under the praise, fluttering his wings enough to lift him off Teman's shoulder, but remaining anchored to the boy's collar. "Are you coming on the adventure?" he asked Sally curiously. "Tay is going to reason with the dragon."

"Shh!" Tay whispered nervously. "I told you, the others wouldn't understand."

"Understand what, Teman?" Sally cocked her head.

The boy felt himself blush. "I suppose it's silly really," he muttered, "but I don't think it's sportsmanlike to slay the dragon without hearing its side of the story. When Master Vela told me that dragons are intelligent beings that can talk—"

"You decided to convince it to behave itself?" She frowned skeptically. "Do you really think that's possible?"

"I don't know, but it's only fair to try. Perhaps it simply doesn't understand what it is doing."

"I think it is very brave of you to want to try," she remarked.

Teman felt himself sit a little taller in the saddle, and they rode on in companionable silence.

When the sun began to set that evening they stopped to make camp near the further edge of Parrot Wood. Most of the day had been spent riding through the green trees, and Teman decided the forest's reputation was exaggerated. He had seen nothing more wicked than a scolding tree squirrel, and the shady path beneath the trees had been cool and pleasant to follow.

He was feeling so confident that he volunteered to collect firewood while the others set up camp. Leaving Dart in Sally's keeping, he walked a little ways into the trees to search for fallen branches.

As soon as he was fully within the wood, he sensed a change in the atmosphere. Being on horseback while riding through daylight was one thing, walking on foot in the gathering twilight was another.

He felt as if there were eyes watching him—from the tops of the trees, from the thick stands of brush, from the ivy-twined branches. He could sense them all around him. Swallowing hard, he focused on the task at hand, forcing himself to choose carefully and find wood that would burn well.

As he reached for a stick to add to his collection, something reached out and slapped his hand. Tay jumped back, dropping his bundle of wood, which scattered in all directions.

"Here, now! What do you think you are about?" cried a furious little voice. "You leave my bench alone, you great oaf!"

Standing in the shadow of a tree edging the path was a tiny woman dressed all in green and brown. Her full skirts were almost as wide as she was tall, and the top of her head was well below his knee. She stamped one little foot, fists balled on hips. "You Big Folk think you can just take anything you like!" she continued angrily. "Look what a mess you've made of my garden!"

He looked down at his feet and saw he had accidentally trampled a bed of miniature flowers shaped like stars. "I-I'm sorry, ma'am," Tay stammered, jumping back onto the cleared path. Going down on one knee, he straightened the crushed posies as best he could. "I didn't see them there."

"Big Folk never see anything," she mourned, sinking down beside the flowerbed and tenderly adjusting a stem here and there. "You'd think those big eyes of yours could see twice as well instead of half as much!"

He sat down on the path and studied the little figure more closely. Her skirt and blouse were artfully fashioned of supple leaves, their green and brown color composed of an infinite variety of blended shades. Her hair swung to her waist in two long braids, and was of a rich autumn brown—with just a hint of green. Her flashing eyes were hazel, now brown, now green as the light caught them, and her cheeks were flushed with the crimson of her anger.

"Are you a fairy?" he asked hesitantly.

"Do I look like a fairy?" huffed the odd little lady, busily tidying her garden.

"I don't know, ma'am. I've never seen a fairy."

"Well, the answer is no. I do not look like a fairy. Fairies are silly, flighty little things with wings always darting about getting into other people's business. I am a wood sprite. We are the caretakers here. We are in charge of going along after you Big Folk and other intruders and putting the forest back to rights." She brushed her hands together then folded arms across chest. "I have been following you and the other Big Folk all day cleaning up after those great animals of yours. They crush the plants, scatter the leaves, bend the saplings back... You have no idea what a great lot of trouble it all is."

"I am sorry, Mistress—"

"Rowan. My name is Rowan. And you are?"

"Teman, my lady Rowan. Is there anything I can do to help you with your work?"

Rowan's eye softened, and her lips curved in a slight smile. "That's the first time a Big Folk ever offered to clean up after himself. Maybe you aren't as useless as you appear. You could gather some rocks to outline my garden—perhaps that way it won't be stepped on next time."

Teman hurried to collect a handful of smooth pebbles, which he lay around the borders of the flowerbed, slipping a few of the roundest ones into his pocket for Sally's sling. Sitting on the bench that had originally been the subject of their conversation, Rowan idly swung her feet. She was wearing shoes made of acorn husks. "You are different from most Big Folk," she commented at length.

"What do you mean?" he asked, sitting back and running one grimy hand across his forehead.

"Most Big Folk can't see or hear us, even when we do speak to them. You must be a friend of Magic."

He shivered that she should sense it, when he hadn't even known himself until last week. "I am apprenticed to the wizard Velachaz," he answered.

"Ah," she said, dimple appearing in tanned cheek, "the terribly wicked. Was he with you today? If I had noticed him, I would have stopped to say hello. I was more concerned with that terribly loud fellow on the big black horse."

Teman propped elbows on knees, chin in hands. "That is his nephew, Galen. We are helping him on a quest to win his knighthood. He goes to slay a dragon."

Rowan sprang to her feet with a little cry. "What has the dragon ever done to him? Really, that is too cruel of you! Why must Big Folk feel the need to go around slaying anything that moves?"

"Well, it is a very large dragon, and it has burned down several villages near its lair."

"Perhaps it had good reason! Did you ever think of that?"

"Actually, I am hoping to get a chance to ask it that question."

She stared at him, mouth dropping into a little "o" of surprise. "You mean you aren't going to slay first and not ask questions later?"

"I think it only fair to talk to it."

"You really are an exceptional boy. Even most of the Little Folk don't stop to consider that creatures like dragons have feelings too. There may be a logical explanation for the whole misunderstanding."

"I promised a friend that I would at least try to reason with the beast before Galen hacks its head off or—more likely—is fried like a sausage."

"You are a very brave lad, Master Teman," Rowan breathed, hands clasped in admiration. Suddenly, she clapped excitedly, and reached into the pocket of her skirt. "I will give you a present!" She pulled out a shining silver ring as big around as her head, and held it out to him with a little bow.

"Thank you," Tay murmured softly, not wanting to hurt her feelings, but doubting seriously that the ring would fit even his smallest finger.

"Don't worry. It is a Magic ring. It will expand to fit, and continue to adjust as you outgrow it. Put it on."

He hesitated. As many stories as he had heard of magical gifts, there were just as many tales of cursed objects.

Rowan laughed like a tinkling brook. "I promise it won't bite you."

With a sheepish grin, Tay slipped the ring onto his right hand, examining it in the fading twilight. He couldn't see very well anymore, but it appeared almost as if there was a spider-web thin line of glowing gold inset in the narrow silver band. "It is beautiful."

"It is a ring of Fairy Sight. Close your eyes."

Teman did as he was told, feeling a little foolish.

"Now, open them!"

When he opened his eyes, he started backward— for all around him, peeking out of the brush, perched on the rocks, and clinging to the trees were Rowan's fellow sprites. Here and there he caught the flashing wings and high-pitched giggles of true fairies—and even saw the round black eyes of a water pixie peering at him from the bottom of a puddle beside the path.

Rowan crowed delightedly, "Now you will be able to see all the Little Folk, and understand their languages— for not all of us can speak the Big Tongue. They will know you are a friend, and come to your aid when you truly need it. Be careful, however—do not call unless the need is great—for the Little Folk are quick to anger, and do not take kindly to being falsely summoned."

"Thank you," he gasped in wonder. "It is a precious gift, indeed." Then his face fell. He had nothing to give her in return, and he had already ruined her carefully tended flowers. "Oh, wait…I know!" He untied the horn drinking cup he wore at his waist, and dug a small hole beside the flowerbed. Burying the cup in the ground, he packed the dirt up around it, and carefully filled it with water from the pixie's puddle.

Rowan clapped her hands once more. "A reflecting pool! Oh, thank you, Teman! It is just what the garden needed." She sat on her bench and called over one of her fellow sprites to study the pool with her. They whispered excitedly behind their hands as they stared at the water with rapt attention.

All at once, Tay heard distant voices calling his name. "Oh, my! It's getting very late, and I was supposed to bring the firewood. Rowan—"

He turned back to her, but she was gone. He glanced around him, but all the Little Folk had disappeared. There was a small pile of kindling lying in a neat bundle beside the path, and as he scooped it into his arms, he saw Sally coming through the gloom to fetch him.

"Good-bye, my friend Rowan," he whispered.

"Grant you good fortune, Teman," came her voice on a breath of breeze—along with a fading ripple of laughter.

With a final glance at Rowan's garden, and an admiring peek at his new ring, Teman hurried forward to meet Sally.

CHAPTER 6

Castle in the Snow

Teman sat staring into the fire, hugging knees to chin. His mind's eye conjured visions of the forest sprites he had seen gathered around Rowan's garden. He smiled to himself over his newfound secret.

"What deep thoughts are you thinking tonight, my boy?" came a soft voice behind him, and he felt Vela's hand on his shoulder. He looked up at the wizard with a smile as Velachaz sank heavily to the ground beside him.

"About what a wonderful world we live in, Master, full of such mystery."

Vela's hand moved to rest over his, covering the fairy ring. "I see you've been among the fey."

"Aye, I met a sprite in the forest."

"It is a marvelous gift that you have been given, Tay. Guard it well."

He looked down at the ring shining in the firelight. "I will."

Vela patted his shoulder. "And now, get some sleep. The others have been dreaming for an hour, and we must get an early start tomorrow."

"How much further must we go?"

"A day, two at most."

"And then what?"

"Then we shall see. Go on, now."

Tay nodded, and got to his feet. "Good night, sir."

"Good night, lad. Rest easy."

Teman moved across to his bedroll, looking back over his shoulder to see Velachaz staring pensively into the dying fire.

The morning dawned cold and gloomy, with glowering gray clouds that threatened to spit snow at them. Tay was grateful for his warm green cloak—until he realized Sally was shivering in her thin dress and bare feet. "Here!" He wrapped it around her slim shoulders. "You will freeze to death."

"What about you?"

Teman shrugged. "I am used to it. You haven't been living outdoors like I have."

"The boy is right," frowned Velachaz. "Forgive me, Sally—I wasn't thinking. We must see what we can do for you. I can't afford to have my star pupil turning to ice on me either." The wizard went over to the packhorse and poked among the bundles on its back. "Ah, this will do!" He reached into the bag and pulled out a corner of soft sky-blue fabric. He murmured the words of a spell as he pulled, and the fabric grew and grew, until he held a full-length wool cape, which matched the green. "Here, my dear." He handed the cloak to the girl, who took it, eyes filled with wonder.

"Is it really for me, sir?"

"For you. Now, give Teman back his, and we will see what we can do about some boots." He conjured a pair of knee-high suede boots that fit her perfectly.

"Thank you, my lord!" the girl cried, throwing her arms around his neck gratefully.

Velachaz stepped back a step in startled surprise, then hugged her awkwardly. "It is my pleasure, my dear. Welcome to our family."

Tay noticed with a frown that the creation of the clothing had been a strain for the wizard. The Magic was a hard one, and it had left him weak.

"Sit and rest, Master," the boy urged, moving to Vela's side.

"No, Tay. We must be off. I will get plenty of rest along the way. After all, I will merely be sitting on the mare's back while she does all the work."

Teman could hear the edge of exhaustion beneath the light words, and he made Vela mount and watch while the three young people quickly cleared away the rest of the camp. They were soon ready to ride, and as Tay swung up behind Sally on the packhorse, the first snowflakes began to fall.

"It will be a long cold day," Galen observed, kicking Ducky gently into movement.

"Where's Dart?" asked Teman anxiously, realizing for the first time he hadn't seen the little dragonfly since dinner the night before.

"He's here," Sally replied shyly, showing him the creature curled like a kitten in the bottom of her apron pocket. "I thought he might be warmer there."

"A wise thought." Teman smiled.

"Come, let's get started. If we're not careful, the snow will delay our journey longer than we'd planned," warned Vela, waving them to follow Galen, who was nearly out of sight in the swirling snowfall. "We don't want to have to sleep in the open, but there's only one place I know to shelter between here and our projected destination, and it is quite a distance."

"Aye, Master Vela," Tay acknowledged, kicking the sorrel forward. "We're with you."

They rode into a world of drifting white feathers. Tay closed his eyes for a moment and concentrated. When he opened them again, he could see hundreds of tiny figures playing hide-and-seek among the snowflakes, all dressed in white and crystal, and singing merrily in tinkling, bell-like voices. He spent the rest of the morning watching them dance, and trying to hear the words of their songs.

The plodding way north was difficult for Galen to bear, as was becoming obvious from his increasingly short temper. He was, as he so often put it himself, "a man of action," and the slow pace of the horses as they picked their way through the snow, with no trace of adventure in sight, was boring him.

"I say, Uncle Vela—perhaps I should ride ahead a bit and see if I can find anyone who has actually witnessed any of the dragon's dreadful deeds," he ventured after lunch.

"If you think it would help," replied Vela solemnly, the merest twitch of a smile playing about his lips, "but I think you should take Teman with you. Sally and I will continue on along the road, and you boys can go explore."

Tay was secretly as ready for excitement as Galen, but he didn't want to leave Vela alone. "Do you think that would be wise, Master? What if—?"

"I am quite capable of taking care of myself, dear boy," Vela reassured him, "and it will give Sally and I a chance to discuss what she wishes to do with herself if we survive this quest. Run along and have fun."

Tay swung up behind Galen on Ducky. "We won't be gone long, Master Vela," he promised.

"Take your time, lads. Just don't stray so far from the road that you can't find it again. There is an abandoned town at a crossroads some ten miles up the road. We will make camp at sundown. If you are not back before then—look for us there."

"Right," Galen agreed, eagerly turning Ducky's head away from the broad beaten road. "We'll be back!" With a cry of encouragement, he kicked the horse into a gallop, and they flew away into the unbroken white wilderness of the fields.

Tay clung to Galen's waist for dear life, thrilled by the speed of the horse, but rather worried by the fact that the snow hid all the imperfections of the ground. "Galen!" he shouted into the wind rushing past his ears. "Should we really be going quite so fast? What if Ducky should trip?"

Galen laughed, eyes sparkling with exhilaration. "Ducky will be all right. He's spell-protected, you see."

That explained a lot. Teman imagined Velachaz had probably taken the precaution long ago—when he first realized Galen's clumsiness could lead to disastrous consequences for horse and rider both.

"But don't you think it would be easier to find what we seek if we slow down?" the boy asked, taking a different approach.

Galen reined in slightly, pulling the big black stallion into a canter. "You could be right about that," he admitted.

"By the way, what are we seeking, exactly?"

"I don't know...some charred ruins, an abandoned farm, flattened fence posts. Actually, all I really wanted was to get away from the monotony of the road. I'm on a quest!" The young knight struck one of his gallant poses, and almost threw them both off the horse's back. "It isn't supposed to be boring," he mumbled.

Teman sighed with good-natured exasperation. "Well, how do you suppose people get from one place to another? Fly?"

"Well, actually, that was one reason I wanted to have Uncle Vela come along. I thought perhaps—"

Tay realized with a sudden flash of insight that Galen probably didn't know about his resistance to Magic. Even though Vela very likely had the power to whisk them from one end of the island to the other, he wouldn't have been able to use his spells to help the knight, so he preferred to let his nephew think him weak rather than hurt the youth's pride.

Teman's admiration for his master went up another notch. It was awfully unfair that the rest of the world never bothered to find out the truth behind the myth of the "terribly wicked Velachaz."

"Look there!" cried Galen, breaking into Tay's thoughts to point across the snowy plain. Far in the distance loomed a towering pile of stones. They were set more or less on top of each other in such a way as to suggest they might once have formed a castle, but the gaps in the walls promised cold lodgings if anyone still dwelled within. "Perhaps we will find an answer at yonder keep."

Rather doubting as much, but willing to keep an open mind, Tay nodded. "Should we see?"

Galen needed no further encouragement. He wheeled the horse's head, and they sped toward the ruin.

Pulling up before the castle with a showering spray of snow, the knight called out loudly. "Hallo—in the stronghold—is there anyone about?"

With a knife-sharp intensity that made him gasp, Teman felt a warning of danger lurking within the shattered walls. "Galen—" he began, but got no further.

Out of the empty doorway stepped a tall slender woman dressed in a flowing green dress. Her black hair rippled down her back like a silken waterfall, and her face was breathtakingly beautiful. "Well, well, what have we here?" Her voice was musical, holding barely suppressed laughter.

Galen slid from the horse's back to land with a flourishing bow at her feet. "Good day, my lady."

"Good day to you, sir. What is it that brings you to my door?"

"We seek information regarding a dragon that has been reported in the north. Have you been distressed by such a beast?"

Her laughter slipped its leash and spilled into the frosty air. "My, my. Such a noble goal. Won't you step inside and discuss it?" the lady purred, her green eyes glowing like a cat's as she ran a delicate white hand along the young knight's arm.

"Galen—" Tay warned uneasily. Ducky pawed the frozen ground and snorted.

The woman shifted her focus to Teman, and a surge of fear raced through him at the anger smoldering in those gleaming emerald depths. "And who might this be?" she growled ominously.

"This is—"

"Simon." Tay blurted out. Galen looked at him with a puzzled frown but thankfully didn't correct him.

Teman's mind whirled, trying to remember everything Velachaz had told him about Magic, and every legend he'd ever heard. Everyone knew that the easiest way to gain power over another was to know his or her true name. She couldn't charm Galen—Galen was immune to the effects of Magic—but he didn't have that protection himself.

He would have to be very careful.

"Well, Simon..." He felt a stirring of thought at the edge of his mind, and let a silly grin blossom on his face. He knew that she would expect him to be charmed, so he must pretend to be. "Why don't you come down from there and come inside?"

He slid from Ducky's back, and followed the lady and Galen into the ruined tower. Within the crumbled walls was very powerful Magic indeed. Despite the fact that there were huge gaps in the stone structure, it was warm and dry within the room. Tapestries depicting fantastical adventures hung about the walls, some of them suspended in mid-air. A crackling blaze burned in a fire pit centered in the floor, and thick cushions lay around it invitingly. "Come and sit down, boys. Let us talk."

Teman let himself be led to a cushion, still pretending to be under her spell. Sinking onto a soft pillow, he closed his eyes, and concentrated.

Opening his eyes, he gave an involuntary cry then clapped both hands over his mouth with a gasp of horror at what he'd just done. But it was impossible to check his reaction at the sight revealed by the fairy ring. Instead of the beautiful woman she appeared to be, the creature was vaguely cat-like in features, with a mouthful of sharp fangs, and skin like green scales covered with sparse fur. Her long talons were secured wrapped around Galen's arm, but at the sound of Teman's cry, she turned those glowing eyes in his direction. They were narrowed suspiciously.

He forced himself to grin back at her. "Forgive me, lady. I sat on a sharp stone."

Finally, she gave Galen her full attention once more, and Teman searched his memory for some solution. He wasn't sure what the creature was, but he was sure that none of his fledgling spells would be a match for Magic this strong. Velachaz would look for them eventually, but he would have no reason to think anything was wrong for hours. They weren't expected back until dinner.

"So tell me about this dragon of yours, Galen." She sank gracefully onto the cushions, pulling the knight down beside her. Stretched out along the padding, she looked even more like an animal to Tay, and he was not surprised to see the tip of a tail flick out from beneath the hem of her dress. How could they get away from her?

Galen appeared to be having no such concerns about their hostess. He chatted easily about the dragon and the difficulties it had caused farmers in the region. Tay found himself wondering what exactly it was that Galen saw when he looked at her. If he could not be charmed, how could she appear as anything but herself? But if Galen saw her true form, how could he speak to her so matter-of-factly?

Teman shuddered, staring into the fire so that he didn't have to look at her. It took him a moment to realize that she was speaking to him.

Her eyes narrowed to slits as she repeated her question. "As I was asking before, Simon—what say you of killing this dragon?" The sneer in her voice made his blood run cold. She knew. He could tell that she knew.

He gulped. "I-I believe we should reason with it first, mistress. I am told that dragons are intelligent creatures. It isn't right to slay another living soul without a hearing. Even a dumb animal deserves respect—much less a noble beast." His voice became more sure as he talked, for he spoke from his heart.

There was a flicker of grudging approval in the creature's eyes. "Well said, boy."

"I think it's a silly notion," scoffed the knight. "A dragon exists to destroy. Everyone knows that."

Tay forgot his fear of the creature in anger over Galen's attitude. "No—everyone assumes it!"

"Oh, Teman—" Galen began.

The creature suddenly snapped to attention. Tay felt as if time had frozen between one breath and the next. He stared back at the creature as she chuckled evilly. "Ah! Teman, is it? I have you now—"

Galen had no idea what he had done. He continued his sentence as if he had not been interrupted, "...you just don't have the slightest understanding of how the world really works."

"On the contrary, little knight," purred the creature. "Teman knows a great deal about how the true world works, more than you will ever understand. Teman knows quite well." Her eyes were now glowing like bright green stars. They caught his attention and pulled...drawing him down...drowning him. He fought against the pull of those eyes, as a swimmer fights a river current. His lessons hadn't gone far enough. He couldn't draw on the Magic for help! He knew he would be sucked under her control and lost. There was nothing he could do!

"Well, we really should be going now, Tay," Galen commented, clapping a hand on Teman's shoulder. "Uncle Velachaz will be wondering where we have gotten to—"

"Velachaz!" hissed the creature. The light in her eyes snapped out, and she drew back against the wall. "What is Velachaz to you?"

"He's my uncle," replied Galen, leveling a cold stare at the creature. "And Teman is his highly valued apprentice. Uncle Vela is very fond of the boy." There was a very clear threat implied by the remark, and Tay peeked up at the knight in surprise. This Galen was not the clumsy boy he had come to know. This coolly calculating young man had struck fear into the creature with the single weapon they had to use against her. Perhaps Galen going up against the dragon was not so hopeless after all.

"Leave here—now!" spat the creature, pointing a taloned hand toward the door. "Do not come this way again."

Galen bowed low to the creature, "Good day to you, my lady. Thank you for your hospitality. Come, Tay. We must be off." Throwing his arm over the younger boy's shoulder, he led the way back into the snowy afternoon.

Teman glanced over his shoulder as Galen helped him up onto Ducky's broad back. He thought he could see the faintest glitter of green in the gloom of the interior, but there was no other sign of the creature.

"Well, that was close," Galen commented, as he turned Ducky back toward the road. "Perhaps that is enough adventuring for today."

"I think that might be wise," Teman agreed.

"You know, personally, I like my cats small and furry instead of green and scaly," Galen called back to him as Ducky galloped over the snow toward their expected meeting with the others.

Teman's mouth dropped open in shock. Galen had seen her, but never so much as blinked an eye. Yes, there was definitely hope against the dragon. Now—if only he could convince the knight to at least try talking to the beast before he attacked it.

CHAPTER 7

Meeting Mad Elaine

The boys soon caught up with the others. By unspoken agreement, not a word was said about their adventure in the castle. Galen told Vela only that they had seen evidence of the dragon's fury, and it was true—on their way back to the road, they had crossed several areas of blackened landscape, stark against the white of the snow. An orchard that had once borne apples had been reduced to charred and twisted ruins. More than one farmstead had been burned out, the gutted farmhouses trying to hide their wounds under a cloak of snow, which only served to make the damage more obvious.

Teman wondered what had happened to the families that had lost these homes. Had they, too, fallen to the dragon's anger, or merely been forced to move on? It was too quiet. Compared to these empty wastes, Farlea was a city teeming with people. It made it even easier to understand why Galen had been so impressed with the town.

"Do you see yon mountain?" asked Galen, pointing unnecessarily toward a towering crag that rose in the distance. "That is the home of the dragon."

"How do you know?" Sally wondered.

"Well, where else would it live?" he replied grumpily, angry that his grand announcement had been challenged.

"Oh...I see. Scientific reasoning."

71

Before Galen could continue the argument, Velachaz broke in smoothly. "You very well could be right, Galen, for dragons favor such places. However, we need a little more confirmation than that fact. Shall we seek out someone to ask? Sally, you and Teman look in that direction." He gestured east, and they nodded, slipping from the horses to the snowy ground. "Stay together and be cautious, my children. Anyone who is likely to be brave enough to remain in the shadow of the dragon will be unafraid to use force to defend what they hold dear. Do not expect an open-armed welcome. Return here before dusk. We will camp here in the remains of that inn across the way."

"Aye, Master." Tay nodded solemnly. As they walked away from the others, he glanced over at Sally. Her cheeks were flushed with temper, and her eyes snapped.

"You mustn't mind Galen," he said softly, "he isn't as sure of himself as he wishes to sound."

She was quick to anger, but her temper cooled as easily. She shook her head, grinning back at him. "I know it. But he is so irritating! So high and mighty."

"I suppose this quest is a very hard thing to bear, don't you? If he fails, his family will be ruined, and he will likely be dead."

Sally paled. "I hadn't thought of that."

"Well, you can be sure that he has—whether he admits it or not. How old are you, Sally?"

She had taken Dart out of her pocket and was fussing over the little creature. Now, she looked over at Teman, obviously puzzled by the apparent change of subject. "Fifteen. Why?"

"Galen is not yet eighteen. How would you feel in his place?"

They walked on in silence, looking for signs of life. Dart danced around their heads, landing first on Teman's shoulder and then Sally's. After a moment, Sally reached out and stopped him with a hand on his arm. "How old are you, Teman?"

"Near thirteen."

"And how did you become so very wise so very young?"

He blushed, unsure if she was serious or teasing him. "You learn quickly on the streets, Miss Sally."

"Too quickly, I fear," she answered softly. "What's that over there?" She pointed to a low hillock of mud with a wisp of smoke—barely visible against the gray of the clouds—rising from the top of it.

He shaded his eyes and looked where she pointed. "I think it is a house of some kind. Perhaps there is someone inside who can tell us what we need to know."

"It's worth asking. Come on." She ran toward the little hill, Dart following after her.

Teman opened his mouth to offer a word of caution then shrugged. She was halfway there already, and it would obviously do no good to warn her. One thing she shared with Galen was a headstrong determination to do things her own way. All he could do was catch up to her, and hope for the best.

By the time he reached Sally, she was knocking on a low wooden door sunk into the muddy hill. As he fought to catch his breath, the door opened a crack, and he could see one bright brown eye staring out at them. He was reminded uneasily of the cat creature.

73

Sally curtseyed and addressed the form within the house. "Good day, my lady. May we speak with you?"

"You are, aren't you?" came the brusque reply.

"Well, I thought maybe we might come inside. It's awfully cold out here."

"What do you expect when you wander around in the snow?"

Teman found himself fighting to hide a smile. Sally was trying very hard to be friendly, but the woman in the hill quite obviously wanted nothing to do with them. "Come away, Sally. The lady is busy, and we mustn't take up her time with foolish talk about dragons—"

"Wait a minute, boy! Did you say dragons?"

He took a step nearer to the doorway. "Why, yes, Mistress. We have come with a champion who seeks to vanquish the beast." Dart landed on his shoulder with a little squawk of protest, and Teman batted at the dragonfly impatiently. "But he wishes to make sure where it lies in wait before venturing forth."

"Come inside, boy," ordered the woman, opening the door wider. "And you too," she added over her shoulder to Sally. "I can't have you freezing to death on my doorstep."

They stepped under the low doorway and down a pair of steps into the main room of the house. The dwelling was carved out of the inside the hill. The walls rising to a domed ceiling over their heads were packed earth, and decorated with living greenery and flowers that twined around picture frames and furniture in brightly colored patterns. The furniture itself was all very low to the ground, made of rough wood and covered with hand-woven cushions. Dart flickered over to light among the ivy, curling up like a resting cat to watch the proceedings with a solemn stare.

Their hostess gestured toward a settee curving along the far wall. "Sit. I'll make tea."

Now that they could see more of her than one glaring brown eye, their hostess was revealed as a tiny woman scarcely taller than Teman himself. He closed his eyes and concentrated, opening them cautiously, but her appearance was unaltered by the ring's magic. She was still a stout little woman with round red cheeks and untidy hair of a dark rich brown fighting to escape its fastenings. Her clothes were green and gray, and her movements were quick and birdlike as she moved about the house. She reminded him of an old owl that once lived above the stables in Farlea.

Teman led the way to the sofa, feeling rather as if he had stepped into a dream. While they waited, he studied the pictures on the walls with interest. They were marvelous paintings of fantastical beasts. Here was a gryphon rearing back on its mighty haunches with its wings almost seeming to wave in the air as it faced a charging unicorn whose sharp horn glittered menacingly. There a phoenix bird screamed aloft from a bed of fiery ashes. On the far wall, a basilisk glared from the head of a stone statue, surrounded by other frozen figures. But the place of honor over the mantel was held by a large portrait of a soaring red dragon, which spat fire down on clustered huts beneath it.

He looked more closely at the painting then rose with a startled cry to see if his suspicions were correct. Standing before it, with the heat rolling toward him out of the fireplace, he could almost believe he was present at the dragon's attack—for the mean collection of houses falling under the flame was this very town. He was sure of it!

"You have a good eye, boy," murmured the woman at his elbow, handing him a steaming mug of tea. "That is indeed our little town."

"Did you paint this?" he asked in awe.

"Aye, lad. I painted them all. I paint what I see."

Sally turned from the painting of the basilisk. "You saw all these things? How could it be you were not turned to stone by the basilisk's stare?" She pointed toward the gryphon and the unicorn. "Or gored by the unicorn? These are not animals one goes up to and pets like dogs. These are fairy beasts."

"And your point is?" The little woman's voice was mild, but Teman could hear an edge of anger beneath the calm words.

"Why should they appear to the likes of you?" scoffed Sally. "These are the beasts of legend. They would not waste their time with an old woman."

Teman's own temper began to rise at the arrogance of Sally's tone. "You and Galen are just alike," he murmured. "You think you are experts in the ways of Magic, that you know the behavior of the fey. Whatever gave you that idea?"

He turned his back on the girl's surprised expression, and took the woman's rough little hand in his own. He bowed low over it. "This is the hand of a true artist, Mistress. You have a rare talent."

"Thank you, my boy," she replied with a pleased little nod. "Now, you wished to know about the dragon—"

"As if you could truly—" Sally began.

"Sally, go and find the others," ordered Teman, turning to her abruptly. "I will speak to this good lady and meet you back at the camp."

Sally opened her mouth to protest, but he simply stared back at her, too angry to trust himself to speak further. With a huff of annoyance, Sally left the low house and stormed off into the snow.

"I'm sorry about that, my lady," he apologized. "She is not schooled in the Way."

"But you are, my boy. I sense a great Magic within you. My name is Madeline. Mad Elaine the townsfolk call me. And you are?"

Teman was honored by the trust Madeline showed in giving him her true name when she knew he was touched by Magic. He could scarcely do less in return. "My name is Teman. I am apprentice to the wizard Velachaz. It is his nephew that seeks to slay the dragon." He put forth a finger and touched the picture of the dragon.

"And you, Teman. What do you seek?"

"He will convince it to give up these evil ways," chirped a little voice confidently.

Teman looked up in surprise then relaxed. He had forgotten about Dart during the confrontation with Sally. Now, he held out a finger, and the little dragonfly swooped down to perch sedately on the improvised branch. "Dart has great confidence in my abilities," he explained, a trace of laughter in his voice. "Myself, I'm not as sure."

Madeline petted the little creature on its shining head with a callused fingertip. "But it is noble indeed of you to try, Teman. Most folk fear the dragons so much that they do not even try." She sank down onto the settee, and gestured for him to sit beside her. "Do you know that there are less than ten dragons left in the world? They can live to be a thousand, but people have been killing them off for so long that the remaining handful have gone into hiding. This one here," she pointed up at the painting, "is the youngest and the strongest. It is little more than a hatchling. It came to live in the cavern in the mountain less than twenty-five summers ago. At first, no one even knew it was there. It behaved itself and left the townsfolk alone. It fished for itself on the coastline—"

"Fished?" Teman interrupted in surprise.

"Yes. It was a great fisherman. I used to watch it dive and sport in the waves." She sighed then continued. "Then one day, a young knight decided he needed a mighty quest. He came after the dragon he had heard lived in the north. While it was out fishing, he invaded its home, and destroyed the cache of eggs he found there. Dragons are long-lived, but they bear few offspring. The three eggs that the young knight destroyed might have been the entire next generation of dragons—it takes four years for an egg to hatch, and these were close to breaking. Can you blame the dragon for going mad when it returned home to find its shattered hopes?"

Teman gulped, and shook his head, not trusting himself to speak. There were tears standing in his eyes at the thought of the dragon's despair at finding its lost children.

Madeline took his hand in sympathy. "It has been ten long years since that black day," she said softly.

"The dragon has destroyed everything it could find. At first, the people rebuilt after an attack, trying to find something stronger to construct their houses— something that could withstand the dragon's flames. But it would swoop down again and burn the new as easily as it had the old. Finally, they grew weary of trying, and moved on. The north is a wasteland now. No one lives above the wood except the fey, and me. My little home is safe enough from the beast, but if your friend goes against the dragon, he will unquestionably die. It is no decrepit creature that can easily be killed with lance or sword, but a fiery young beast, in the height of its strength. It has righteous fury to sustain it. If you cannot soothe its anger, it will never listen to you long enough for you to reason with it, either. What will you do?"

"Teman will talk to it. He promised," Dart replied, patting Teman's cheek with a tiny paw. "Teman is a good lad."

"Yes, I can see that," Madeline replied with a chuckle. "One who inspires great loyalty. But how will you speak to it, Teman?"

"I-I'm not sure, but my master Velachaz says—"

"If you travel with Velachaz, then you must know his secrets."

Teman frowned thoughtfully. How much did she know? "Some of them, my lady."

"Then you know there is little hope Velachaz will help you save a dragon."

"I can only try. I will not see it destroyed without at least trying."

"You are an exceptional boy, Teman. Your heart does you great credit. I would like to give you something." She patted his knee then stood with a heavy sigh, crossing to a tall cabinet against the wall and rummaging through the drawers.

He watched her with a bemused expression. In the last week, so very much had happened to him he couldn't take it all in: meeting Vela, getting a home, becoming a friend to the fey, starting on a quest. Everyone he met, with the exception of the cat creature, had wanted to gift him with something. From having nothing to call his own, he was starting to become quite the man of property.

He came back to the present as Madeline held out a fine gold chain. Hanging from the chain was a large red teardrop-shaped pendant. He took the chain from her and examined the pendant. It was smooth and as hard as rock, yet flexible. When he turned it this way and that in the firelight, it glittered with tiny flecks of gold and iridescent shimmerings. "It is beautiful," he breathed. "Thank you."

"It is a scale from the dragon. It is said that it will protect its wearer from dragonfire. I have never had cause to test this claim for myself, however, so I would not stand too close to the beast despite it. I give it to you as a reminder that the creature is not impenetrable. It does have weaknesses. It can be killed. But it has also been hurt and what has been hurt can be healed. If you can persuade it to abandon its thirst for revenge, you will be doing us all a great favor."

He slipped the chain over his head. The scale glittered against his rough brown tunic. "I will do my best, Lady Madeline."

She smiled at him. "Just keep that head of yours attached to your shoulders. Too few children your age know how to use theirs. Be careful, Teman—and may Fortune walk beside you."

Teman bowed low to the artist, then hurried off to meet the others. Dart buzzed around his head in the late afternoon sunlight, and Tay could almost see the real dragon's raid on the village as he watched the little dragonfly flitting about.

It must have been an awesome sight, despite the destruction—the huge red wings beating in the sun, the great lances of flame thudding into unprotected roofs. All inspired by grief for its children. How can it be blamed for its reactions?

The closer he got to camp, the slower he walked. He didn't know what course to take. Normally, he would ask Velachaz for advice, but when it concerned dragons, how could the wizard be objective? On the other hand, he couldn't stand back and let Galen attack the creature when it had been acting out of grief and rage.

Teman came to a decision. He veered away from the road, and headed toward the distant mountain. If he returned to the camp and waited until morning to go with the others, he wouldn't get a chance to reason with the beast. It was now or never.

CHAPTER 8

Up Close and Personal

As the sun sank in the west, sending spears of golden light to gild the treetops, Teman slogged through the snow toward the distant mountain. At first the walk was exhilarating, and the honor of his cause kept him moving toward his goal. Dart flit from side to side of the road, wings catching the sunlight in flashing sparks of gold. The little dragonfly hummed to himself as they walked, too excited to settle down and carry on a conversation.

The mountain was further than he had expected. The wind blew cold on his face and hands, and soon his exposed skin felt numb. But he had committed himself now, and it was too far to turn back before dark. The light was nearly gone when he neared the forbidding tumble of rocks at the base of the mountain. Tay began to question the wisdom of his impetuous decision to come alone.

There was a glow of light from amidst the rocks, and he went toward it cautiously. Peering around a boulder, he saw a large cavern running back into the depths of the mountain. The light was coming from firelight reflecting off crystals embedded in the walls of the cavern. The firelight was coming from the dragon.

It lay curled like a dog in a pile of greenery on the cavern floor, snout resting on front paws. It appeared to be asleep. With every breath, twin puffs of smoke rose from its nostrils, and a tiny flame spurted from its mouth. Occasionally, some of the greenery would blaze up, and the dragon would swat at it absentmindedly without waking and put it out.

Teman stood behind the boulder with Dart perched on the rock face above him and watched the creature sleep for some time. He hated to wake it up, but didn't want to waste the chance to talk to it either...and the flickering flames drew him like a moth to a candle. It would be warm inside.

He had inched forward to confront the beast when he stepped on a bit of icy rock, and his foot slipped out from under him.

"Watch out!" squeaked Dart in alarm, taking to the air. The little dragonfly fluttered around Teman's head as the boy pinwheeled his arms wildly, fighting for balance. Tay lost the fight with a startled cry, and fell flat on his back, staring up at the night sky, now spangled with pinpoint stars. The fall knocked the breath out of him. He lay dazed by the impact, but the damage had been done.

A terrible bellow erupted from the cave. Teman scrambled to his feet, his heart frozen in his throat as he stared at the scene before him.

The dragon reared back, mighty talons raking the air. Not yet fully grown, it still grazed the cavern ceiling with its crest, a good twenty feet above Teman's head. It was awe-inspiring: horrifying, yet glorious. Its scales were ruby-red rage and gold-dust glitter, and a spiky ridge ran from the base of its head to where its tail ended in a wicked barbed point. Its eyes gleamed angrily as it glowered down at him, and wisps of steam hissed from its nostrils with every breath. Each of its claws was as long as a dagger, and the flickering firelight glinted off a mouthful of fangs. Teman felt his knees give beneath him, and Dart hid behind the boulder.

"Who dares disturb my slumber?" roared the dragon. And its terrifying image was shattered. The voice should have matched the cruel exterior. Instead, it was high-pitched, plaintive—and female.

"Why, you're a girl!" whispered Teman in astonishment. Somehow, despite Madeline's story, he never realized the dragon might be female. It made the loss of the eggs much worse.

The dragon's willowy neck snaked down to bring its eyes level with his own. "What business is that of yours, boy? Be gone, before I boil your blood and bake your bones!"

Teman swallowed hard, but met the dragon's big black eyes squarely. "I don't believe you would do that."

The dragon chuckled wickedly, showing a mouthful of very sharp fangs. "Perhaps you are right. Why waste a perfectly good snack? I'd sooner just eat you raw!"

"Well, then—eat me," answered Tay, lifting his chin bravely.

"W-what?" The dragon backed away a step in surprise.

"I said, go ahead and eat me. If you are going to do it anyway, I would rather you just got it over with, please. It is frightfully cold out here."

The dragon frowned. "Aren't you going to beg me to leave you alone, or run in terror?"

"No, actually. I'm too tired to beg, and too cold to run. So, if you are going to eat me, let's just get it out of the way."

"I can't just eat you in cold blood. What kind of creature do you take me for?"

"I've heard that you are a blood-thirsty beast who has been burning and pillaging everything in sight, but I don't think it is true." He shivered a little, pulling his warm cloak more tightly around him. Even the thick wool couldn't keep out all the chill as the wind began to rise.

"Don't stand there freezing, boy! Come inside." The dragon retreated a little further into the cave, leaving Teman a space to get in out of the cold. She breathed onto the pile of greenery, and it blazed up, creating a crackling fire. He warmed his reddened hands before it gratefully.

"Thank you," Tay murmured politely.

"You are welcome. Please, sit down," she said shyly, waving a foreleg at a rock beside the fire. "Not many people come to visit me."

He settled himself comfortably on the rock. "Perhaps they are afraid," the boy commented.

"Of course they are afraid!" snorted the dragon indignantly. "I am a fierce dragon! They are wise to be afraid!"

"How can they fear you and come visit you? I don't think you can have it both ways."

"Then I'd rather be feared."

"You don't mean that," Tay said softly. "I think you are very lonely up here in your cave."

"What do you know of being alone, boy?"

"A great deal. It isn't much fun, is it?"

The dragon sighed, and lay down in a miserable heap, snout resting on paws once more. "No, it isn't."

"I'd like to help."

"How could you possibly help me..."

"Teman. My name is Teman, but my friends call me Tay."

"Am I your friend?"

"I'd like for you to be, my lady—"

"Fieriluna," she answered softly. "It means Fire Moon."

"That's a beautiful name," Teman observed with a smile, reaching up to scratch behind her ear.

Fieriluna purred like a kitten. "That feels good."

"I don't think you are half as wicked as you would like people to think Fieriluna, but you certainly have been trying to live up to your reputation."

"What do you mean?" she asked, swiveling her great head to face him.

"You are old enough to know better! Your behavior has been terrible. You've been burning people out of their homes, setting their fields on fire."

"They started it!" she cried heatedly, rising onto rear legs. "They dammed my stream and took away my drinking water. Then they tried to seal me up inside my mountain. I didn't want to hurt anyone, but I had to defend my home. And when I was out fishing one day, they—" The great beast stopped, unable to continue.

Tay stepped closer to the dragon, leaning backward to look up into her face. He murmured, "Someone smashed your eggs. So you struck back at them and destroyed the things they held dear in return. But the farmers didn't kill your babies, Fieri."

The dragon nodded vigorously, her big head bobbing up and down. "Yes! They did! I wanted to hurt them back but it didn't change anything—my babies are still dead."

"A woman in town told me that it was a knight on a quest that destroyed your eggs, not the villagers. This is all some huge mistake on everybody's part."

Fieri whimpered. "I'm tired of fighting now. I would simply like to be left in peace. I could go back to my fishing, and be happy. Only, now I don't know how to make things right. People will never listen to me." The tears that had been gathering in her black eyes spilled over, splashing Tay from head to toe as they hit the stone floor like buckets of thrown water. "What do I do now?" she wailed.

Teman stepped forward, patting her awkwardly on the leg. "Don't cry, please, don't cry. My master Velachaz will help you. If anyone can set this right, he will."

"I don't see what anyone can do to put things back now."

"I know that nothing can replace your eggs," he murmured, "and I am sorry for that." Tay continued to pat the dragon's flank in what he hoped was a comforting manner. The scales were soft and warm under his hand—not at all what he expected. "People have a tendency to fear what they do not understand, and to lash out against what is different. But there must be something that we can do—"

The dragon moaned, lowering her great head onto her forepaws once again. "It's no use. I might as well leave the island...but it's my home. I was hatched in this very cavern—"

There was a blur of wings, and Dart fluttered up to rest on Teman's shoulder. "Don't do anything foolish, Teman. I appreciate your trying to help, but it isn't worth getting hurt over. You promised to talk to her and hear her side, and you did, but things have gone so far—"

"Well, I can't just give up without trying! And it isn't fair for Fieriluna to lose her home any more than it was right to burn the farmers out of theirs. The only way to begin to change things is to make everyone—on all sides—listen to the truth. Master Velachaz will know what to do. I can't sit back and let Galen attack her or let her destroy him in self-defense either. The first thing we have to do is get back to the village," he stated firmly. "For one thing, they will be wondering where I have gotten to."

Tay bowed low to the dragon, as his mother had taught him to do before a lady. "I am most pleased to have made your acquaintance, my Lady Fieriluna, but now I must be getting back to camp." He thought of the cold dark tramp ahead of him and shivered.

"Could I take you there?" she offered shyly. "It is not very far to town if you fly."

Teman's heart sang. To fly! And on the back of a dragon, no less. "That would be wonderful."

Fieriluna laid flat, her neck stretched along the ground. "Here," she directed, "put your foot on my leg and swing yourself up. Lie flat along my neck, and wrap your arms around it as if it were a tree."

Teman did as he was instructed. His arms weren't long enough to go completely around her neck, but he held on as tightly as he could.

She twisted her head around to face him. "Don't worry," promised the dragon, "I won't go very fast, or fly too high. You won't fall."

"I trust you," Tay replied solemnly, digging his knees the best he could into the scales on either side of her neck. Her skin was warm and supple, and he felt very safe, despite the danger of his perch.

"Are you ready?" she asked.

He nodded, too excited to speak. He was going to fly!

There was a rush of air behind him, and he clung more tightly to the dragon's neck as the great wings beat again. Dart settled into the hollow of his shoulder and sheltered against his throat.

Slowly and majestically, Fieriluna rose into the starry sky. The ground below them fell away until all Tay could see was a solid white blanket of snow beneath him. He laughed aloud as the frosty air knifed past him. Now, this was truly Magic! Wait until the others saw her.

The thought sent a tingle of dismay through his pleasure. How was he going to make Galen listen to her story before he chopped Fieri's head off? And could he ever convince Velachaz to trust a dragon...

CHAPTER 9

Tit for Tat

Flying high over the snowy plain, Teman was filled with wonder. He saw the distant tumble of stone that marked the cat-creature's castle. It appeared much closer when seen from the perspective of flight than it had seemed on horseback. He could even see the edges of Rowan's wood, and wondered how the sprites were faring in the snow. Fieriluna had been right that it would take them no time at all to fly from the mountain to the village. The trip was all too short for Teman. Especially when he thought about what he was likely to find at the end of it.

Mad Elaine's cottage was on the far edge of the village as they circled in to land. He almost asked the dragon to put him down there, both to show Madeline the creature, and to avoid confrontation at the inn, but he knew he would have to face Velachaz sometime. He might as well do it now.

The dragon gracefully spiraled down into an open field beside the abandoned inn where Vela said they would set up camp. Teman hugged Fieri's neck tightly. "Thank you," he said simply, not knowing how to further express the emotions the journey had aroused in him.

"You're welcome, friend Tay," she replied, with a shy duck of her great head. "It was my pleasure."

Before Tay could say anything further, the door of the inn burst wide, and a shaft of light spilled out of the opening. Velachaz loomed in the doorway. "Is that you, Teman?"

Teman's heart sank. He had rarely heard the mage's voice sound so cold, and never before when speaking to him. "Aye, Master Velachaz."

"Where have you been all this time?"

"I-I went..." Tay felt a puff of warm breath on his back, and drew courage from Fieri's presence. "I went to see the dragon."

The inn courtyard was suddenly lit by one of Vela's lightning bolts, and Fieriluna reared up in alarm with a startled bellow. The roar brought Sally and Galen at a run. Galen had his sword drawn, and Sally held a guttering torch.

"My stars," breathed the wizard, staring up at the great beast. Sally nearly dropped the torch at the sight of her.

"This is my friend Fieriluna, Master Vela. Fieri, this is—"

Fieriluna cowered behind Teman as best she could, which wasn't very well. "Don't let them hurt me, Tay," she begged him.

"Don't worry," he whispered soothingly. "No one will hurt you. I will protect you."

"It's a girl!" murmured Sally, holding the torch higher and studying the dragon with interest.

"So it is," replied Velachaz distractedly, taking a step closer to peer up at Fieriluna with a puzzled frown. "So it is."

Galen gulped and raised his sword in a trembling hand. "Stand fast!" he cried, his voice coming out as a pinched squeak. He cleared his throat and tried again. "Stand fast, you evil beast, and face your doom!"

The great head swung toward the would-be knight, and two great plumes of smoke rose from her nostrils. Sally jerked Galen's arm down and moved between him and the dragon.

"Don't be silly, Galen! Can't you see how scared she is?" She turned to Fieriluna and stepped closer. "He won't hurt you, Miss. I won't let him."

"Sally—" protested Galen.

"Hush!"

Vela examined the dragon critically in the dim light of the torch. Suddenly, he sank down on a rock with a thud.

Tay was beside him instantly. "What is wrong, Master?"

"It's her. She was the one."

"What do you mean? The one who what?"

Vela's eyes grew cold. "The one who did this to me." The wizard raised his right hand as far as he could. "The one who ruined my life."

The boy shivered. "I'm sure Fieriluna would not hurt you on purpose. How can you be sure she was the one?"

"See that scar on her wing?" Vela jerked his chin toward the dragon. A pale white line ran diagonally across the cap of her right wing, barely visible in the light of Sally's torch. "That is from my dagger. I gave it to her the day she attacked me."

The dragon's long neck snaked down, and she peered closely at the mage sitting on the rock. There was a sudden startled puff of steam, and then she scrambled backward away from the little group before the inn. "Don't let him hurt me, Tay!" she whimpered once more.

"Me hurt you?" Vela snorted, lurching to his feet. "Look what you did to me! How can I hurt anyone?"

The dragon covered the cap of her wing with a sharp-taloned foot. "You hurt me before. I remember."

"You attacked me!"

"Wait. Master Velachaz, what exactly happened?" Teman asked breathlessly.

"I was examining a dragon's egg, and it hatched. Before I could move back, this creature attacked me—"

"How did she attack you?" the boy persisted.

"What do you mean how? She ran up and slashed at me with her claws."

"Are you sure she was attacking? Maybe she was just being friendly and didn't realize her own strength. After all, she was just a hatchling—" Teman was sure he had hit on the truth of the matter.

"And I reacted by striking out at her with my dagger—"

"Which made her slash back at you all the harder."

Vela sank back down on his rock with a hollow laugh. "All this time I have blamed the dragon, and it was really all my own fault."

Sally laid a hand on the wizard's shoulder. "It wasn't anybody's fault. It was simply a misunderstanding."

"Oh, dear. I didn't mean to," murmured the dragon, her big eyes swimming in tears. "I just thought you were playing—and then you cut me, and I got angry. I didn't know you were hurt."

Velachaz studied the dragon thoughtfully, massaging his crippled shoulder. "What a lot of trouble can come from a simple misunderstanding."

He reached out tentatively and stroked the dragon's silky nose himself. "Poor little thing."

"How can we put things right, Master Vela?" asked Sally, planting her torch in a crevice between the rocks.

Galen threw down his sword in disgust. "This is ridiculous!" He pointed at the dragon. "Even if she didn't intend to hurt you, Uncle Vela, that wicked beast is responsible for all the destruction we found on our way here. For the burnt out farms, and the ruined crops, and for the homeless families—"

"Her eggs were destroyed first, Galen!" Teman cried, rushing to Fieriluna's defense.

"What right did that give her to burn their homes?" snapped the knight in reply.

Sally slapped him. Hard.

"What did you do that for?" Galen complained, raising a hand to his cheek.

The girl's eyes blazed with anger. "How could you be so...so cold? What would you have done in her place? If the farmers had killed your babies?"

"Well you didn't have to hit me!"

Teman ignored the squabbling young people and knelt at Vela's feet. "Could you set right the damage, Master Vela? Help the farmers rebuild?"

"It would take more Magic than I can control alone, my boy. The spell is an extremely powerful one." Vela waved his hand expressively.

"There is a spell that would help?"

"If the farmers would accept it, the help could be given. But repairing the damaged buildings will not entirely heal the breach between the people and the dragon."

"If anyone can help Fieriluna, you can, Master Vela."

"Thank you for the vote of confidence, my boy," murmured Vela, "but how do you propose I do that? I am not all-powerful, my boy, despite what the superstitious may say."

"Couldn't I help you?" Tay asked eagerly, placing a hand on Vela's knee.

Vela gazed down into the boy's eyes. "Perhaps you can, lad. How much are you willing to risk?"

"W-what do you mean?"

"As I say, it is a powerful Magic. Such Magic can burn as well as heal. I would need to draw on your strength and send the power back through your fingertips. It might cost you very dear."

Teman peeked over at the dragon then took a deep breath. "I-I understand, Master. But I want to try. I have to help her. I promised."

Vela smiled down at him, like a dazzle of sunlight. "All right, my boy. We'll try it. First thing tomorrow, but for now, let's get some rest," replied Velachaz, rising awkwardly to his feet by leaning heavily on Teman's shoulder.

"You can stay with me at the cavern, friend Tay," offered the dragon shyly. "It's warm and dry."

"May I, Master Vela?" Teman was eager for another opportunity to fly.

"If you wish, my boy, go ahead."

"I can't believe you—" Galen started, but at a glare from Vela, he shut his mouth with a snap. Stiff with offended dignity, he scooped his sword from the dirt. "I'm going to see about the horses."

"I'll come with you," Sally stated firmly, retrieving her torch.

"I don't need your help." He stalked toward the makeshift stables housing Ducky and the others.

"I'm coming anyway, so you might as well be nice about it." She ran after him, the torchlight dancing along beside her.

Vela stood before the dragon. She raised her head until her eyes were level with his, and stared back at him gravely. "I realize that you will be taking a great risk to help me, Master Velachaz, and you have no reason to do so, and every reason not. Thank you."

"We will talk more tomorrow," Vela said. "Safe journey, Mistress Fieriluna." He bowed low before the dragon. "Behave yourself, Tay. I'll see you both bright and early."

Teman swung onto Fieri's great neck once more. It was beginning to feel quite natural astride the dragon's back. He looked for Dart, but the dragonfly was nowhere to be seen. He shrugged to himself. The little creature was probably off with Sally.

"Good-bye, Master Velachaz," murmured the dragon, with a nod of her head. She beat her wings, and they soared up into the cloudless sky. The stars seemed almost close enough to pluck like apples.

With a final dip of her wing, Fieriluna turned for the cave, and Teman snuggled into her warm scales, thrilling to the feel of her mighty wings carrying them through the night.

The next morning Teman awoke as the sun rose. The first rays peeking into the cavern touched sparks of crimson from Fieri's red-gold scales. The mighty dragon was still sleeping, and he studied her in the warm golden light. It was easy to see why she inspired terror in the farmers. Full twenty-five feet long from snout to hindquarters, with another fifteen feet of spiked tail, she was a formidable creature. Anyone who simply saw her, without getting to know that the ferocious exterior masked a gentle heart, would be terrified of her. And the farmers had never bothered to make her acquaintance, but merely struck out against her.

Velachaz would remedy that. Teman had every confidence the wizard could convince the farmers the dragon did not have to be feared. And when he and his master had restored the land, everyone could live peacefully together.

He was sure the dream could become a reality. With the absolute faith of the very young, there was no doubt marring his certainty.

Fieriluna's big eyes blinked sleepily, and she gave a mighty yawn. "Good morning, friend Tay."

"Good morning, lady."

She spread her wings, the outstretched tips touching the walls on either side of the cavern. "Today we shall set things to rights. Do you think the farmers will forgive me, Tay?"

"Especially if we restore their lands. If you are willing to forgive them, I don't see why they shouldn't forgive you. Yours was the graver hurt."

"Can Master Velachaz really set things right? I have heard he is a most powerful wizard, but a spell such as that..." Fieriluna's voice died away.

"If anyone can do it, it is he," replied Teman confidently. "Shall we go back to the village?"

"Is it safe? It was dark last night, but if the farmers see me, they may bring out their bows and spears."

"I'll protect you," Teman promised recklessly.

With a nod, Fieriluna knelt so that he could climb upon her back. As soon as he had mounted, she took to the air, and they were soon spiraling into the inn yard. Tay caught sight of Mad Elaine as they came in to land. She stood before her house, shading eyes with hand as the mighty dragon flew above her. Teman waved, not knowing if she could see him or not.

Madeline waved back, and started for the inn. Teman crowed, "She saw me, Fieri! Now she will be able to come and meet you."

Fieriluna puffed out an agitated cloud of steam.

She is afraid to meet new people, and one can hardly blame her, but Madeline respects dragons and other fey creatures. It will be all right. After all, we won't always be here for Fieri. Someday, we will have to return home, and the dragon will be able to use a friend like Madeline.

Fieri landed in the dirt inn yard, and Sally ran out to meet them. She stroked the dragon's shimmering scales in welcome, and as Madeline appeared, Teman introduced the artist to the beast. Then he turned to Sally. "Where are the others?"

"Master Vela is trying to reason with that stubborn fool Galen. He still believes that he must slay the dragon to fulfill his quest. He refuses to acknowledge that the king will be perfectly happy as long as Fieriluna stops torching the countryside and eating the livestock."

"I had better go and see if the master needs me," said Tay thoughtfully, excusing himself, and leaving the womenfolk to talk. He stepped into the gloomy interior of the abandoned inn, and peered into the darkness, looking for his master.

"I think this is a bad idea, Uncle!" Galen shouted from a shadowed corner. "The king did not ask for compromise. He wants that beast dead!"

Teman followed the sound of Galen's voice, coming up on the pair just in time to hear Vela say softly, "There has been enough killing, nephew. If that arrogant knight had not butchered Fieriluna's eggs for his own quest, this destruction could have been avoided. If we do not help her now, how are we better than she has been? It is better to teach by example than force. And she is truly sorry for what has happened."

"Aye," Tay added. "She was only trying to defend herself."

Vela turned at the sound of his voice. "Ah, so the two of you are back. Are you sure you are ready for the task ahead, Tay?"

Teman nodded. "I'll do anything you say, Master."

"Right." Vela clapped his hands together. "Come, we will have a council of war." He threw an arm around Tay's shoulder, and the boy helped the wizard out into the sunlight, pretending that he was not supporting a good deal of Vela's weight as they moved.

Teman watched Velachaz anxiously as they walked out of the shadowy inn. There were deep lines of care on the wizard's face, as if he had slept badly—if at all— and the streak of silver at his right temple had widened. This quest was taking a heavy toll on Velachaz. The boy hoped it was not too much for the wizard. Where was the legendary power his master was said to command?

"Greetings, my lady," murmured the mage to Fieriluna. "How are you this fine morning?"

"Anxious, Master Velachaz," the dragon replied solemnly. "Do you really think you can help me?"

99

"It will not be easy, and it may drain us both, but we will try."

The council of war met in the inn yard. Fieri curled against the wall of the inn. Teman and Sally leaned back on her warm belly. Vela was once more ensconced on his rock, looking frail and wan. Refusing to participate in the discussion, Galen sat scowling with arms folded and back to the assembly.

Vela addressed the dragon solemnly. "Mistress Fieriluna, the knight did you a grave injustice when he destroyed your eggs. I can understand your pain. However, I doubt that the farmers will understand that this has all been a series of misconceptions. Have you any suggestions as to how we can make them listen to the truth?"

Fieri's big eyes brimmed with tears. "I've tried, but they only throw things and shoot sharp pointy sticks at me."

"Perhaps I may offer a suggestion?" Madeline shuffled into the courtyard, leaning upon a carved wooden staff. Vela made as if to rise, but she waved him back. "Sit, lad. You look done in."

Teman bounded to his feet and dragged forth a stump from the woodpile for her to sit on. She nodded her thanks, and sank onto it with a little grunt.

"Please, lady, we would be happy to hear your thoughts," Vela invited.

"You need a way to make the farmers listen, do you not?"

"Yes."

"Do to them what was done to Fieriluna. Steal their children."

"What! Are you truly mad?" Galen exploded to his feet. "What are you thinking? You can't steal their children!"

"Unlike the dragon eggs, I intend to give them back," replied the old woman calmly. "Can you think of a better way to make them listen? It will gather everyone together in one place, and no one will act impulsively for fear of hurting the children. As for the children themselves, they will be thrilled to meet a dragon, and be none the worse for the experience."

Vela pursed his lips, considering the proposal. "It is a drastic step. It could easily rise up like an asp to bite us. However, as you say, it is one guaranteed to make them listen."

Madeline nodded. "Spirit the children to the dragon's lair, and I will gather their parents."

CHAPTER 10

Comes the Spring

Fieriluna bent her great neck and addressed Vela hesitantly. "May I fly you to the cavern, Master Velachaz? I can easily carry you all if you'd like."

Galen snorted. "I'd sooner wrestle a lion with my bare hands. Ducky and I will ride." He stalked toward the stable.

"I'd better go with him," sighed Sally wistfully. "Otherwise he will get lost."

"I will be glad to fly you later, Miss Sally."

The girl's face lit up and she smiled happily. "Thank you, lady!" With a bob of her head, she hurried off after Galen.

Teman helped Vela onto Fieriluna's neck then mounted himself. As soon as the boy was set, the dragon rose into the sky. Tay heard the intake of breath behind him, and turned his head, shouting against the wind. "Isn't it glorious, Master?"

Vela leaned forward to speak into Tay's ear. "It certainly is, Tay. Thank you for sharing it with me."

Teman laughed, turning back to watch Fieri swoop in for a landing. As soon as they reached the ground, he slid from her warm neck and gave Vela a hand.

The mage winced with pain when his bad leg hit the ground. Tay felt the wings of anxiety brush him. "Are you sure that we can do this, Master Vela?"

"We have little choice, Teman. Galen hasn't sense enough to back away unless there is no reason to fight.

The farmers will continue to persecute Fieriluna unless they are made to see reason. And the poor dragon is caught in the middle, not wanting to fight any longer, but needing to defend herself to survive."

"What must I do?"

"The first spell is a simple one. Gathering the children should not prove too difficult. There are few families left in the north, and we do not have to go terribly far afield." Velachaz took a deep breath. "Are you ready?"

Teman nodded solemnly.

Awkwardly going to one knee so that his eyes were level with the boy's, Velachaz lifted his right hand to Tay's shoulder. Beads of sweat broke out on the wizard's forehead, and the lines about his mouth deepened.

"Are you all right, Master?"

"I will be fine." The tight little smile made the words a lie, but Teman pretended to believe him. Vela laid his good hand on the boy's other shoulder. He quirked an eyebrow at Teman.

The boy nodded again.

Velachaz began to speak the words of a spell under his breath. Teman felt the familiar tingle begin to gather in the pit of his stomach. The Magic filled him like he was an empty cup—but it didn't stop when the cup was full.

It is too much! I can't channel it. It burns...

Teman bit back a cry of pain. He couldn't show weakness now. Velachaz was counting on his strength. He threw back his head and raised his arms, throwing the Magic forth as if tossing the contents of the cup. The Magic soared up in a column of blue flame, and

Teman felt a surge of joy burst from his lips in a wild torrent of laughter. Vela's deeper laughter rose to join his, and then came the higher-pitched sound of children giggling with delight.

Teman whirled at the sound. The clearing before the cavern was filled with children, and Fieriluna was letting them climb all over her as she lay across the mouth of the cave. "We did it!" Teman murmured in awe.

"Yes," Vela sighed, his voice a mere whisper. "We did."

Teman turned back to his master as Vela levered himself to his feet, leaning heavily on Tay's strength. The wizard was white as linen, and his hands were shaking.

Alarmed, Teman forced Vela down on one of the tumbled boulders. "Master, you are ill."

"Just a little tired, my boy." Vela smiled. "It is taxing keeping up the illusion of the terribly wicked alone. It drains my minor Magics, and weakens the greater. With your help, that will change."

"Master, wouldn't it be better to tell the world the truth? I will still be at your side, but you will be able to help in public instead of strike fear."

"I can't, Teman. How will I explain the deception?"

"It is a time for truths, is it not? We have told Fieri the truth about the knight and her eggs. We will tell the farmers about why Fieri attacked. Why not tell the world why you have hidden behind the reputation?"

"You are a child, Teman. You do not understand the ways of the world."

"Perhaps I am a child, but I know enough to realize that the deception is killing you. And I am not strong enough to save you alone."

"Our concern at the moment is the dragon. Let me gather my resources. The parents will be here soon."

Teman reluctantly went to help Fieri with the children. There was one little girl whose tears he had to soothe, but the remainder were quite content to play upon the dragon's back.

Galen and Sally thundered into the clearing upon Ducky's back. Sally slid to the ground. "We saw the farmers on the way up the mountain. They will be here any minute."

Vela rose to his feet. "You will have to be our spokesman, Sally."

"I can't do that, Master Velachaz!" the girl protested. "I am no speaker."

"You are the only hope, Sally," said Vela, laying his good hand against the girl's cheek. "Teman is too young. They would never listen to him. Madeline is considered a little mad. And Galen wants nothing to do with the affair."

"But you should be the one to talk to them!"

"I must stay in the shadows until the time is right, child."

"What do I say?" Sally wailed.

"Tell them the truth." Vela smiled. He called the children to him and herded them into the interior of the cavern.

Fieriluna lay down across the entrance of the cave, little puffs of nervous smoke rising with every breath. Teman moved to stand beside her head, scratching behind her ear to calm her. Galen had tied Ducky to a nearby tree, and stood now at the edge of the clearing, pretending not to be interested in anything occurring at the cavern. Sally paced in front of the dragon, wringing her hands and muttering to herself.

The sound of angry shouting could be heard coming up the mountain toward them. Sally froze. Despite his pretended disinterest, Galen moved to stand beside her, his hand on the hilt of his sword. Gulping down panic, Teman stepped up to flank Sally on the other side. The three of them stood shoulder to shoulder in front of the dragon.

A crowd of farmers and their wives armed with bows, spears and pitchforks boiled into the clearing. Sally's hand crept into Teman's. He gave it a reassuring squeeze, and noticed Galen did the same on the other side.

Madeline shoved her way through the crowd to join the trio. "Listen to what they have to say!" she shouted over the din of the farmers.

"Why?" bellowed a huge man. The pitchfork in his hand glittered ominously in the sunlight. "They are just children themselves!"

"They may be children, but they have more sense than you, Nick Plowman!" Madeline scoffed. "Are you afraid to hear the truth?"

"I am afraid of no man nor beast," Plowman growled.

Fieriluna raised her head to peek over Teman's shoulder.

Plowman backpedaled with a little squawk that belied his boast.

"P-please... If you could only just listen for a moment." Sally stepped forward, her earnest little face filled with intensity. "Listen to what happened."

A woman's voice cried out from the back of the crowd, "Where is my baby girl? What have you done to her?" Other voices added their anger to the din.

Sally gulped, twisting her hands before her. "The children are fine. They will be returned to you as soon as you listen."

"Why should we?" Plowman shouted, his courage returning as Fieri made no move to attack. He brandished the pitchfork. Galen's hand tightened around the hilt of the sword. Teman shook his head at the knight with a scowl.

"B-because a grave injustice has been done here."

"Aye! Our children have been taken from their very beds!"

"They are fine!" Sally cried, straining to make herself heard over the sound of the crowd. "Unlike Fieriluna's eggs, no harm has come to them."

"What are you talking about, girl?"

"Fieriluna's children were destroyed before they could hatch. It wasn't your fault, but she didn't know that." Sally gestured at the dragon. "She came home from fishing to find her eggs smashed and her stream dammed. Can you blame her for fighting back? She was angry. Surely you can understand that? How did you feel when she destroyed your homes? How did you feel when your children were taken? That is how she feels."

"We didn't destroy no eggs," Plowman growled. "Why are we being punished?"

"Did you dam her stream?"

"Well...we needed the water for our crops. Especially after that beast burned us out the first time!"

"You dammed the stream before she ever came near your crops." Sally's voice was stronger now. She stood before the farmer with hands balled on hips and snapped back at him, "Did you even think to ask her for permission?"

"It's a monster! A dumb animal."

Fieriluna snorted and lifted her head. "I am not dumb!" she protested, steam puffing from her nostrils.

"It talks!" squealed one of the women, hiding behind her husband.

"Of course I talk," Fieri scoffed. "And I am not an it!"

"What kind of trick is this?" Plowman stepped forward, shifting his grip on the pitchfork.

"It is no trick," Teman called, moving forward himself. "Fieriluna is a mother who lost her babies, just like you. How do you feel right now, when your children have been taken from you? You will get your children back. Fieriluna may never have any others.

"But that is not the reason we called you here."

"Why did you bring us here?" called a man.

"We wanted to make you a proposition."

"Who? You pack of half-starved children? What can you have to offer us?"

"We can restore your lands, if you will let Fieriluna live in peace."

"You and what army?" Plowman scoffed.

A lightning bolt cracked out of the shadowy cave and hit the ground at Plowman's feet. "This one!" thundered Velachaz, stalking out of the cavern.

The crowd shrank back. Whispers ran through the clearing. "It is the terribly wicked Velachaz!"

Vela raised his arms, and thunder roared. Teman murmured the words of the wind spell, and dust devils whirled about the farmers.

"Now, are you ready to listen?" Vela shouted above the crashing thunder.

Plowman nodded, his arm encircling a small woman who wept into her handkerchief.

"Everyone sit down."

The farmers and their women obeyed the command, sinking onto the floor of the clearing.

"I know that you will not be able to truly concentrate on what we have to say until you know your children are safe." Vela gave a piercing whistle, and the children surged out of the cave, running to their parents with shouts of laughter.

The farmers and their wives hugged their offspring to them, murmuring endearments. The children chattered excitedly until Velachaz raised a hand for silence. Instantly, the children quieted.

"Now, let us begin again," Vela purred, nodding his head to Sally.

More confident with the wizard present, Sally began again. She repeated what she had told the farmers about Fieriluna's eggs, and the plan to restore their lands.

"When will this miracle occur?" Plowman's voice held an edge of skepticism.

"At dawn," replied Velachaz.

Teman could not sleep. He sat outside the cave, chin in hands, while the others slept. The stars overhead blazed like diamonds. They made him feel very small.

He kept going over and over the lessons that Vela had taught him that afternoon. His own part was not difficult. Vela would be pronouncing the complex spell. He was merely the channel through which the Magic would flow.

Velachaz limped over to join him, sinking down on the ground with a sigh. "You should be getting some rest, my boy."

"I know, Master..."

"What is it?"

"Do you really think that I can do this?"

"Honestly?"

Teman turned to Velachaz, his heart in his throat. He had expected Vela to reassure him immediately. Am I strong enough?

Vela smiled at him, face shadowed in the starlight. "You are the most powerful Natural I have ever seen, Teman. If you cannot do this, no one can. Not me, not Talthos of Azure City, not Chantara of the Seven Kingdoms. The whole success or failure of our enterprise rests on your shoulders. I need the strength within you. Without you, I will fail."

Teman swallowed hard. "I will do my best, sir," he promised.

"That is all you need do."

The morning dawned crystal clear, sunlight sparkling off the snowy fields. The farmers filed into the clearing before the cavern, and stood like silent statues. Teman felt the flutter of fear in the pit of his stomach and swallowed hard. He must be strong. Velachaz was counting on him. But as he faced the circle of expectant farmers, he was terrified that he did not have what Velachaz sought.

"It will be fine, lad," Vela murmured, his left hand clasping Tay's shoulder. "Remember what I told you."

Teman nodded. He took a deep breath. "I am ready."

"Good. Let us begin." Velachaz led Tay to the edge of the path leading into the clearing. They stood on a rocky bluff overlooking the valley where the village lay. Vela's hand tightened on Tay's shoulder. "Remember what I told you. We have to make this spectacular for them to believe our story. It will be a taxing spell indeed. But if anyone can perform it, it is you."

"I will do my best, Master."

"I know you shall, lad. Let us begin."

Teman raised his right hand. It trembled slightly, and he concentrated on steadying it.

"Don't be ashamed, boy. You have a right to be frightened. I am asking a great deal of you."

"I can do it." Teman steeled himself and nodded. "I'm ready."

Vela's hand tightened on his shoulder, and the wizard began to murmur under his breath. Teman pointed his hand toward the far edge of the valley. He felt the tingling begin to gather, and focused his will on the harnessing the Magic. His heart began to pound. Vela's voice rose in cadence. The Magic began to flow down Tay's arm.

Now! It begins now!

The familiar blue fire arced from his hand to dance across the valley. Slowly, a haze of green began to bloom in the distance, replacing the snow. Inch by inch they spread the growth across the valley. Halfway through it, Teman felt he would not be able to continue.

It is too much. I don't have the strength.

He could feel Vela's hand tighten on his shoulder, lending strength of its own. He straightened his back and closed his eyes.

I can do it. I can do it!

The Magic fountained from his fingertips. He opened his eyes, watching the springtime come into the vale. By the time he reached the far side, his hand was shaking badly, and he could hear the ragged edge to Vela's chant. The last bit of snow melted away under new growth, and he swayed on his feet.

Behind him, Velachaz fell to his knees, nearly dragging Teman down with him. Tay spun on his heel, his own weakness forgotten as he studied his master's face anxiously. Vela's skin was gray paper, and the lines bracketing his mouth appeared chiseled in stone.

"Master! Are you all right?"

"I will be fine, lad," Vela whispered, trying without success to give Teman his normal dazzling smile. "Help me to my feet."

Teman lent the support of his shoulder to Vela, and the wizard levered himself to his feet. Slowly, they turned back toward the clearing. To find the circle of farmers staring at the valley below.

The sound of birds fluttered upon the warm breeze, along with the scent of new-mown hay. They could hear the distant tinny clanking of bells as cattle moved through the fields.

"Will that do?" croaked Velachaz wearily to Plowman. "Will that clear Fieriluna's debt?"

"How long will it last?" asked the big farmer in return. "If the magic fades at sunset, it will do us no good."

"The spell will last as long as a single villager wishes it to. Within this valley will be an endless season of growth until you wish the snow again and all must agree, down to the youngest child. Time will pass from spring to summer harvest and then return." Vela's voice was stronger by the time he finished speaking. "Will that do?"

Plowman glanced at his fellow villagers. There were nods and gape-mouthed wonder from all assembled. "Aye, my lord. That will do."

"And in return, you will leave Fieriluna to fish in peace. To live here on her mountaintop without fear of harm?"

"We promise, lord."

Teman tugged on Vela's sleeve, and the wizard bent to listen. Teman whispered in his ear, "Madeline, Master. Will they treat her better?"

"Ah. Good point, Tay, my boy." He turned back to Plowman. "And no more calling the Lady Madeline 'Mad Elaine.' She is a friend of mine, and under my protection."

"It shall be as you say, my lord."

"Come, Teman. Let us go back to the inn."

Teman nodded. He was very tired, and his right arm felt like thousands of gnats were crawling upon it.

They passed through the crowd of farmers and Fieriluna ferried them back to the inn yard. Sally and Galen bounded out to meet them. The girl's apron was full of flowers, and Galen had a rough wreath of daisies tilted over one eye.

"You did it, Uncle Vela!" Galen shouted, boyish enthusiasm chasing away his knightly arrogance. He caught Vela up and spun him around.

"Put me down, you young pup!" Velachaz scolded with a little laugh. "My brains are addled enough as it is."

Sally handed Teman a flower. "Oh, Tay! The valley is beautiful. It is like springtime. How did you do it?"

"I don't really know myself."

She raised a fingertip to his right temple. "What is this?"

"What do you mean?"

"There is a streak of silver running just here."

Teman drew back and looked at Vela. The wizard tilted the boy's head. "You've got your wizard's mark, my lad. Welcome to the Brotherhood."

Fieriluna snaked her head down between Sally and Teman. "Would you care for that ride now, Miss Sally?"

"Oh, could I?" Sally's eyes glowed like stars.

"I would be honored to carry you." The dragon turned toward Galen, ducking her head shyly. "And you, Sir Galen."

Galen shook his head. "I am not a knight. Somehow, it is no longer important to me that I become one. Madeline has offered to let me work her fields. I will be quite content to be a simple farmer. It is what I wanted all along." He held his hand out to Sally. "And Sally has promised to stay and keep me in line."

The girl blushed.

"Congratulations, my boy." Vela beamed down at his nephew. "This is marvelous news."

A worried frown brushed Galen's forehead. "There is the small matter of the king. He will not be pleased. I do not want him to take his wrath out on the family."

"I shall speak to him, Galen. I am sure he will listen to the terr—"

Teman cocked his head at Vela.

"To the wizard Velachaz." He smiled down that the apprentice. "It appears I will be leaving the terribly wicked role to others. I am sure someone somewhere will take up the mantle. Now, go along you two. I know that you are dying to have your flight."

Galen helped Sally onto Fieriluna's neck, and then mounted behind her, his arms firmly around her waist. Sally grinned up at him.

Teman felt a fleeting wisp of jealousy. They looked very happy.

Dart buzzed up and landed on his shoulder. "Where have you been?" he asked the little creature fondly, reaching up to stroke its wings.

"Here and there. Far and yon. Rowan says hello."

"Will you be staying here with Sally?" He held his breath—a little worried the dragonfly would say yes.

"Don't be silly," said Dart. "I am going with you. I want to see the dragonflies you told me about. The ones who don't talk."

Teman felt his heart lift. At least he wouldn't lose all his friends at once.

Vela waved the dragon on. "Go on with you lot. Teman and I must rest. The spell takes a heavy toll."

The dragon beat her wings and rose into the sky. They could hear the delighted laughter of her passengers as she soared aloft.

"Will the king listen, Master?"

"He is a sensible man and a good ruler. Why, he may even knight the boy anyway. But his main concern was that the dragon stop terrorizing the countryside. That has been accomplished."

Teman shaded his eyes and followed the dragon's flight. "They will be happy, won't they?"

"Aye, lad. They will be happy." Vela looked down at Tay. "And what about you? Will you be happy?"

"Oh yes, Master. To harness that power freely... to mold the Magic... That will make me truly happy indeed."

Vela reached out his left hand. Teman grasped it with his right. He grinned.

Thank You!

Thank you for reading our book and for supporting stories of fiction in the written form. Please consider leaving a reader review on your favorite site, so that others can make an informed reading decision.

Acknowledgments

I would like to acknowledge Wolfgang for helping me out of a dead end plot dilemma, and moving us to a soaring conclusion!

This book owes a great deal to my original mentor at the Institute for Children's Literature, Joanne Hoppe. Without her support, it might never have become a novel after its humble short story beginnings.

I would also like to thank Laura Adlam and the staff at LTD Books who gave it first publication, and Sandy Cummins at Writers Exchange who took up the mantle next. And Michael Wills of Digital Fiction Publishing who let it soar again.

About the Author

Rie Sheridan Rose wrote her first stories in crayon before she was ten. That was a long time ago. She's better at it now. She always wanted to write—if you do too, don't let anything stop you!

Rie lives in Texas with a herd of cats and her husband who helps wrangle them.

The Right Hand of Velachaz is a story where the kid wins, because those are the best stories. It is a story of hope, courage, and dragons. We hope you like it.

Her newly polished website can be found at http://www.riewriter.com or learn more about the Conn-Mann Chronicles at http://theconnmannchronicles.com/

Follow her on twitter at @RieSheridanRose